The one person Cassidy didn't expect to see in the barn examining the newest sick horse was Farley.

"So how is Chickweed doing?" She patted the horse as she walked around him, doing a quick visual exam. "Is he running a fever?"

"Afraid so. And he's definitely suffering some pain— see how swollen he is under his jaw?" Farley placed her hand over the enlarged lymph nod she nodded.

Not only did sh_____ _____ _____ _____ in the horse, but she al_____ _____ _____ _____ ey's hand. And the st_____

She remembered _____ _____ _____ hands had felt like on her waist and on her shoulder, when they'd danced together four years ago. She'd never forgotten and never would.

Did he ever think about the good part of that night?

Or just her inexcusable behavior afterward?

She glanced at his face, and saw that he was looking at her, his dark gaze intense as always, but inscrutable.

He blinked.

The moment between them—if indeed it had been a moment—was over.

Dear Reader,

Welcome back to Coffee Creek, Montana, where the Lamberts—a family of ranchers and cowboys—own the largest spread in Bitterroot County, all controlled by matriarch Olive Lambert. This time Cassidy Lambert takes center stage. With her business degree finally completed, Cassidy plans to get a job in the city and finally win complete independence from her domineering family. But when one of the family horses comes down with an infectious case of strangles and vet Dan Farley puts the ranch in quarantine, Cassidy steps in to help.

The good-looking local vet is considered by many to be the county's most eligible bachelor. Too bad Cassidy burned her bridges with him four years ago. It'll make working together all the more uncomfortable. What happens next seems to be part of Cassidy's mother's controlling plans. Or is it? Please read on, and decide for yourself.

One of the pleasures of writing a family saga is creating the setting for the stories. In this case I took a real town name— Coffee Creek, Montana—nudged it a little in a southwesterly direction, made it the head of fictional Bitterroot County and decked it out with interesting establishments like the Cinnamon Stick Café and the Lonesome Spur Saloon. There's a two-story brick courthouse in the center of town, next to the post office and library. If you'd like to see the pictures that inspired the setting and stories, please visit my storyboards on www.pinterest.com under CJ_Carmichael.

There are more stories coming, so please keep an eye out for *A Promise from a Cowboy* this August, with *Cowboy Christmas* following in October. And do visit my website, where I hold regular contests and chat about my writing process and new stories in the works.

Happy reading!

C.J. Carmichael

www.cjcarmichael.com

Her Cowboy Dilemma
C.J. CARMICHAEL

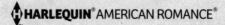
HARLEQUIN® AMERICAN ROMANCE®

Recycling programs
for this product may
not exist in your area.

ISBN-13: 978-0-373-75450-2

HER COWBOY DILEMMA

Printed in U.S.A.

ABOUT THE AUTHOR

Hard to imagine a more glamorous life than being an accountant, isn't it? Still, C.J. Carmichael gave up the thrills of income tax forms and double-entry bookkeeping when she sold her first book in 1998. She has now written more than twenty-eight novels for Harlequin Books, and invites you to learn more about her books, see photos of her hiking exploits and enter her surprise contests at www.cjcarmichael.com.

Books by C.J. Carmichael

HARLEQUIN AMERICAN ROMANCE

HARLEQUIN SUPERROMANCE

*Harts of the Rodeo
**Coffee Creek, Montana
‡Return to Summer Island
***Three Good Men
†The Fox & Fisher Detective Agency

This is for my Aunt Eleanor Schatz, who only this summer reminded me that she was the one who introduced me to Harlequin romances. Thanks for sharing your books—here's one for you!

Prologue

It was strange to think of Brock getting married today. He was the youngest of her brothers and, Cassidy Lambert would have asserted, the least serious and least responsible of the bunch.

Yet falling in love with Winnie Hayes had changed him—in good ways. And at twenty-eight, he certainly wasn't too young for marriage. Not that his brothers had set good examples on that score.

B.J. at thirty-four and Corb, thirty-two, were both still single. Could it be they'd talked Brock out of taking the plunge?

Or maybe he'd come up with cold feet all on his own.

How else to explain the fact that Brock, who was supposed to be the groom, and Corb, who was supposed to be the best man, and their driver, friend and foster brother, Jackson Stone, were fifteen minutes late for the ceremony?

Everything else was in place. Guests filled the pews of Coffee Creek's pretty white church. The organist was doing her best to drive them crazy with important-sounding music. And the bride and bridesmaids—Cassidy included—were waiting in the antechamber for their big moment.

"What time did Corb say they left?" Winnie asked.

She was perched on the ledge of the windowsill with Cassidy, both of them peering out on a warm, sunny July afternoon.

With her dark hair, creamy skin and lovely figure, Winnie made a perfectly gorgeous bride. She was also fun, a good cook and strong enough to set Brock straight when he needed a firm hand.

Cassidy approved.

She also liked Winnie's friend from New York City, Laurel Sheridan, who was checking her watch for the umpteenth time.

"Thirty-five minutes ago," Laurel replied.

"What's happened?" Winnie stared out the window as if she could will the Coffee Creek Ranch's black SUV to suddenly appear.

"Don't worry," Laurel said. "Could be they ran out of gas or had a flat."

"Or maybe they got halfway here only to realize that Corb forgot the ring." Cassidy made the joke halfheartedly. She was actually starting to worry—something both Corb and Brock would tease her about if she admitted it later.

She swung her new cream-colored cowboy boots, admiring how they went with the sage-green dress that Winnie had picked out for her and Laurel. She and Laurel were dressed like twins, except Laurel was wearing pretty, high-heeled pumps with her dress.

Cassidy didn't do pumps. Cowboy boots and running shoes were more her style.

"But if they've been held up," Winnie said, "why haven't they called?"

Laurel held out her hands to Winnie. "You're making me dizzy up there." Winnie jumped, and then Cassidy followed.

"I'll call them," she said, unable to stand the waiting anymore. "I'll go get my phone."

She slipped out of the antechamber, intending to head for the minister's office at the other end of the hall. All three of them had left their purses—including their phones—in the bottom drawer of the filing cabinet.

But a late-arriving guest caught her eye. Dan Farley, the local vet, was as darkly handsome as ever, and the distraction of seeing him unexpectedly like this made her momentarily clumsy. As she tripped over her own feet, Dan gave her a quick, dismissive glance.

Not quick enough, however, for her to miss the disapproval in his expressive dark eyes.

Or was it dislike?

Probably both, Cassidy decided, as she continued down the hall, trying not to think about the broad-shouldered vet or the beautiful woman who'd been standing by his side.

Who was that woman? Her brothers hadn't mentioned anything about Farley having a new girlfriend. She entered the minister's office, went to the filing cabinet at the back and pulled open the drawer.

Then again, why would they tell her? No one had any reason to assume she'd be interested in Dan Farley's love life.

Nor was she. Not particularly.

She grabbed her phone and called up Brock's number. As she waited for him to answer, she made her way back to the antechamber. As she slipped inside the door, she heard Winnie whispering something to Laurel, but she stopped talking as soon as she saw Cassidy.

"Brock isn't answering." Cassidy ended the call, frustrated. "I'll try Corb."

No answer there, either. "Damn."

Finally, she called Jackson. Again, nothing. "If this is some sort of prank, I'm going to kill them."

Actually, if she saw them right now, she'd be more inclined to give them all hugs. She was really worried and—

"Someone's coming!" Winnie was back at the window. "I think it's Jackson's SUV."

Cassidy hurried to Winnie's side. *Please let her be right!* But one glance dashed all her hopes. "No. It's the county sheriff's vehicle."

She looked at Laurel, then Winnie, seeing in their eyes the same fear that was making minced meat of her stomach. They watched in suspended dread as the local sheriff made her way out of her vehicle toward the church.

"Who is that?" Laurel asked.

"Sheriff Savannah Moody," Winnie answered. "She's a good friend of Brock's. We were going to invite her to the wedding, but he said there was bad blood between her and B.J. I don't know the details."

Neither did Cassidy. One of the drawbacks of being the youngest in the family was that no one told her anything. Still, she knew the trouble went back a long time, to the last year B.J. had lived at home.

Cassidy rushed out of the antechamber in time to see Savannah make her grand entrance. The crowd—expecting to see a bride—was quelled at the unexpected sight of the sheriff.

Aware of Winnie and Laurel coming up behind her, Cassidy made room for all three of them to follow in Savannah's wake.

"I need to talk to someone from the Lambert family." Savannah's official-sounding voice lifted and carried through the silent church.

B.J. stood first. "Savannah. What happened?"

Olive Lambert rose next, clutching her son's arm. "What's wrong?"

"I'm s-sorry, Olive. There's been an accident. Jackson's SUV hit a moose on Big Valley Road, about five miles from town."

A collective gasp by the congregation was followed by a few seconds of stunned silence.

Cassidy flashed back to the days when her father had been teaching her to drive. "Always drive slower at dusk. That's when your chances of hitting wildlife are the greatest. And pray that you never hit a moose, Cassie. They're lethal."

"Brock?" Winnie whispered.

Savannah rotated slowly, not having realized the bridal party was standing at her rear. "I'm so sorry, Winnie. Brock was in the front passenger seat—the impact point with the moose. He didn't have a chance."

Cassidy felt as if she'd been kicked in the solar plexus. She was doubling over, just as she heard B.J. ask, "What about Corb? And Jackson?"

"Jackson was driving, wearing his seat belt, and the air bag was able to cushion him from the worst of it. He's badly bruised and shaken, but he's okay. Your other brother was in the backseat. He should have been fine, but I'm afraid he wasn't wearing his seat belt. As we speak he's being medevaced to Great Falls. I can't say how bad his injuries are. You'll have to talk to the doctors for that."

"Is he conscious?" Desperately Cassidy prayed for Savannah to say yes.

But the sheriff shook her head. "No."

Brock, dead. And maybe Corb, too? *No, no, no, no...*

Cassidy wanted to run screaming from the church.

But Laurel tugged on her arm, gesturing to Winnie. The bride was tottering on her heels, shaking violently. Cassidy reached out for her and, between them, she and Laurel managed to keep her from crashing to the floor.

"We need a sweater or a warm jacket," Laurel called out to the crowd.

A second later, a man's suit jacket was settled over Winnie's shoulders, and a white cotton handkerchief was pressed into Cassidy's palm.

She glanced up to see Dan Farley ordering the crowd to step back and give Winnie some space as he swooped the bride into his arms and carried her out into the fresh air.

Cassidy stood back to let them pass, her hand fisted over the handkerchief. Farley must have given this to her. Only then did she realize that tears were cascading down her face.

Chapter One

Ten months later

What did it say about her relationship with her family that the person Cassidy Lambert was most excited to see when she got home wasn't a person at all, but her border collie, Sky?

Sky had been her father's birthday surprise for her fourteen years ago. Sky was loyal, loving and, most important, *uncomplicated*. Cassidy knew, no matter what, that Sky would always love her and think she was the most wonderful person on the planet.

The same could not be said of her family.

Cassidy lowered the driver's side window of her vintage 1980 Ford pickup to let in the warm spring air, then cranked up the tunes as she barreled along the 80 toward home. She knew she should reduce her speed, not only to avoid a ticket but also to prolong the drive, which she was quite enjoying.

But she was on a high. After five long years she was finally done with late nights at the library, relentless assignments and tough exams. She'd worked hard to complete the Accounting Master's Program at Montana State University, but she'd done it, and hopefully soon would follow a high-paying job at one of the top accounting firms in Billings.

Josh Brown—her friend and would-be boyfriend if she could make up her mind about that—also had plans to move to Billings. Josh had wanted to come with her to Coffee Creek Ranch. He said it was time he met her family.

"I wouldn't be so anxious if I were you," she'd told him. He thought she was teasing, but she wasn't.

"They can't be that bad. Look at you. Unless you were adopted?"

"No such luck." She had her mother's delicate features and the long, lanky body that came from the Lambert side of the family. She had a soft heart—like her father. But was also headstrong and stubborn—like her mom.

Yet despite all the family resemblances, she'd always been a misfit. Part of the problem came from being the only girl in a family with three boys—four if you counted her foster brother, Jackson, who'd been with the family since she was nine. She knew it wasn't her imagination that her mother was harder on her than the guys. And her father had treated her differently, too, when he was alive.

For one thing, he'd built three cottages by the small lake on their property for each of his sons to live in. But nothing for her.

No doubt he'd expected her to one day get married and go live with her husband. But being excluded that way had hurt.

And it still did.

The boys had been relentless teases, too. They didn't mean to be cruel, but they never cut her a break, either. Even though she could ride as well as any of them, she couldn't match them in strength. And, oh, how they'd loved to taunt her about that. Especially Brock…

Tears fogged her vision, and she slid her sunglasses up on her head so she could rub them away. Though almost a year had passed since the accident that had taken her youngest brother's life—just an hour before he'd been about to marry Winnie Hayes—the loss still felt fresh.

Brock may have driven her crazy, but she'd loved him, living in hope that one day he'd stop treating her like a bratty little sister and they might become friends.

Now they would never have that chance.

Cassidy drove over a series of three gentle hills before arriving at the smattering of buildings and the weathered sign proclaiming that she'd arrived at the town of Coffee Creek. She put on her indicator light, intending to stop at the Cinnamon Stick Café for some fortification before continuing the last fifteen minutes to the ranch.

It was Wednesday morning, the last week of April, an hour before noon. She'd written her final exam the previous afternoon, had spent a night on the town with all her friends, including Josh, then loaded her car for an early departure that hadn't included breakfast.

So she was hungry.

She angle-parked in front of the pretty café that was owned by Brock's former fiancée. Winnie had taken Brock's death really hard and had gone to live at her parents' farm in Highwood immediately following the funeral. Cassidy stayed in touch with her via Facebook and knew that Winnie hoped to return to Coffee Creek eventually. Apparently she'd developed some health issues that weren't serious, but required some time to settle.

In the meantime her café was being operated by Winnie's best friend—and Cassidy's new sister-in-law—Laurel. Laurel Sheridan had flown in from New York for Brock and Winnie's wedding and had ended up extending her stay to take care of Winnie's café while her friend was convalescing. She'd also fallen in love with Corb and the two had been married last September in New York City.

Then in March they'd had a baby—adorable little Stephanie Olive Lambert was another reason Cassidy was stopping at the Cinnamon Stick. Hopefully Laurel and the baby would be there.

She was dying for a cuddle with her new little niece.

Cassidy parked, hopped out of her truck, then paused to stretch her back and her arms. One thing about older trucks—they sure weren't built for comfort. Still, she patted the hood affectionately before heading toward the café.

A hand-painted sign hung over the door, and two wooden benches promised a place to sit in the sun and enjoy your coffee once you'd placed your order.

Inside she was welcomed by the scent of freshly ground coffee beans and the luscious aromas of butter, sugar and cinnamon. She'd come during a lull and the place was quiet. Two older women sat at one of the two booths, engrossed in conversation. Behind the counter, Laurel was softly singing a silly song about hedgehogs. She had her back to the door, busy with dishes, but she spotted Cassidy's reflection in a carefully positioned mirror and broke into a big smile.

"Cassidy! You're home!" Laurel stopped to scoop up her two-month-old daughter from the playpen. "Look who's here, Steph. It's your auntie Cassidy."

Cassidy was already holding out her arms for the bundle. "I hope she isn't making shy yet."

"Oh, she's still too young for that. Besides, she's getting used to new faces. We just got back to work last week and I swear our business has tripled. It seems everyone in the area is finding an excuse to drop in for a coffee and to say hello to the newest Lambert."

Cassidy listened to all of this with a smile, at the same time noticing how happy her sister-in-law appeared. Pretty, too. Her long red hair was pulled back in a ponytail, but it seemed thicker and glossier than ever. And her fair skin was literally glowing.

Laurel deposited a kiss on Cassidy's cheek as she handed over her daughter, who had gained several pounds since Cassidy had seen her last.

"Oh, you're so cute! Look—she has Corb's dimple."

"I know. Isn't it adorable? And only on the left cheek, just like her dad."

Cassidy sighed as Stephanie cuddled in, soaking up the smooches that her aunt couldn't resist planting on her downy soft head. Her wispy hair was coming in orange. And curly.

"How are you doing, precious? Do you like working with your mommy in the café?"

The baby looked up at the sound of Cassidy's voice, and Cassidy was amused to see that she had the Lambert green eyes, as well. Stephanie was staring at her intently, and only when she raised her little hand, awkwardly reaching up, did Cassidy realize she was entranced by the sunglasses that were still resting on her head.

"She's just started noticing her hands a few weeks ago," Laurel commented. "Sometimes she stares at them for minutes at a time. It's so cute. But here I am, talking endlessly about my wonderful baby, again." Laurel rolled her eyes. "What's new with you? How were your final exams?"

"They went well, I think. I won't have my marks for a few weeks."

"Can I get you a coffee and a cinnamon bun for the road?"

Hearing the door open behind her, Cassidy moved out of the way so the newcomer could enter. "You read my mind, thanks."

"Make that a double order, Winnie," said a deep voice behind her. "And leave some space for cream in the coffee."

Cassidy *knew* that voice. Slowly she turned, holding Stephanie like a shield between her and the tall, broad-shouldered man who'd just entered the café.

Sure enough, there stood Dan Farley. The local vet had some Native American blood, which accounted for his high cheekbones, jet-black hair and dark, almond-shaped eyes. Though he'd spoken to Winnie, it was Cassidy he was looking at, with cool dislike.

"Hey, Farley." Darn her voice for coming out so soft and weak. She lifted her chin. "How are things?"

"Busy."

He knew she'd been going to college in Bozeman, and must have noticed the suitcases and boxes in the back of her truck, but he didn't ask about her studies or show any interest in whether or not she was moving back to Coffee Creek. Stepping past her as if she were nothing more than an inanimate obstacle, he made his way to the counter, where he pulled out his wallet.

Heck and darn, but the man had a way about him. Cassidy glanced at the two women at the back to see if they felt it, too. Sure enough they both had their eyes on Coffee Creek's sexy vet. One of them pretended to fan her face with her hand. The other laughed and winked at Cassidy.

Cassidy didn't wink back.

He wasn't *that* good-looking.

She gave him another glance, seeing only his profile and long, muscular build.

Okay, maybe he *was* that good-looking.

Still, he probably hated her and she had only herself to blame.

Winnie set two coffees in to-go cups on the counter, then bagged them each one of the homemade cinnamon buns baked fresh every day by ex-bronc rider Vince Butterfield. A veteran of the rodeo circuit and a member of the Cowboy Hall of Fame, Vince had licked a lifelong dependence on alcohol and in his sixties had begun a new career as a baker. His mother's old recipe for melt-in-your-mouth sticky buns, thickly topped with frosting, was his new claim to fame.

Five minutes ago, Cassidy had been craving one of them desperately. Now her stomach churned at the thought. What were the chances that she and Farley would happen into the café at the same time? Pretty darn slim. So slim, in fact, that she hadn't run across him here once in the past four years.

Other than at the church last July, she hadn't seen him anywhere else, either.

If he was called out to the ranch when she happened to be home, she always made herself scarce. She'd avoided him at the funeral. If his name came up in conversation with her brothers, she tried not to listen.

And now here he stood, just a few feet away. Making it very hard not to remember… But no. She would not think back to that night. She couldn't bear it.

"So where are you off to now, Farley?" Laurel asked, her tone friendly. Everyone in the Coffee Creek area called the vet by his last name. Probably to avoid confusion with his father, also named Dan, whom he'd worked with before the elder Farley and his wife had retired to Arizona.

Farley glanced briefly at Cassidy again, before answering. "Coffee Creek Ranch."

Though there were plenty of reasons why the vet might have been called out to her family's ranch, Cassidy's first thought was for Sky. At fourteen years of age, every day was a blessing. "What's wrong?"

"Your mother's young palomino is sick. Sounds serious."

"Lucky Lucy? Oh, no." She was glad Sky was okay, but this news was almost as bad. Her mother had bought the beautiful three-year-old palomino just this year and Cassidy loved her. Lucy had a wild heart but a gentle soul. Though she was her mother's horse, Cassidy had felt a special connection with the mare from the first time she'd ridden her.

"Any idea what the problem is?"

"From the symptoms Jackson described, sounds like strangles."

"Really?" In all of her twenty-five years they'd never had a case of strangles on the ranch. She didn't even know that much about it, other than it was a highly contagious, serious infection of the nose and lymph nodes.

"I'll have to examine the horse and run some tests to be sure." He added a generous amount of cream to his coffee, fitted the cup with a lid, then grabbed one of the bagged cinnamon buns. "See you later, Laurel. And thanks."

No word to Cassidy, whose ranch he was heading for.

She might as well be an empty bar stool for all the attention he'd paid to her. Wordless herself, she watched as a half-dozen long strides took him out the door.

The café fell silent then, and Cassidy realized that Laurel was looking at her, eyebrows raised.

"What's up with you and the vet?"

Cassidy shifted Stephanie to her other arm. She'd planned on staying for a while to visit, but the bad news about the ranch had her suddenly anxious to get moving again.

"Why do you ask?"

"Are you kidding? Sparks were flying here, and they weren't the good kind. Farley isn't the chattiest of people, but I've never seen him be downright rude before. And the way he all but ignored you? That was rude."

Yes. It sure had been.

"I guess he figures he has his reasons." Cassidy went around the counter to deliver Stephanie back to her playpen. She didn't seem very happy about being set down until her mother wound up a musical mobile that had been affixed to the side of the playpen.

"How do you get any work done with such a cute distraction around?" Cassidy bent to give her niece one last kiss.

"It's taken some adjusting, by me and the staff. Eugenia and Dawn have been great. And even Vince has taken a few turns at rocking Stephanie when she's being fussy."

"That I'd like to see." Vince was the epitome of the tough, silent cowboy from another era.

"I know. Isn't it amazing what babies bring out in a person?"

"It sure is." Though Farley hadn't seemed moved by the baby at all. Of course, if she hadn't happened to be there, he probably would have been much friendlier to Laurel and her daughter. "Is there anything I can do to help you before I leave?"

"We're fine," Laurel assured her. "Eugenia's shift is starting in about half an hour. That'll give me a chance to take Stephanie upstairs, feed her and put her down for her nap. She's a great sleeper, thank goodness. Gives me a couple free hours every afternoon."

"Sounds like a good system." Cassidy counted out money for her order, then picked up her drink and her pastry. Now that Farley was gone, her appetite was returning. "I'd better get going."

"Wait one minute. You're really not going to give me the scoop on you and Farley?"

"Nope." Cassidy gave Laurel a warm hug. "I'll be back to have a longer visit in a few days. Or I may drop in on you and Corb at the ranch one evening."

"I'll look forward to it. But be warned. Next time I see you, you better be ready to tell me what's going on with you and the vet. He's considered the most eligible bachelor in town, you know."

Cassidy wasn't surprised. The guy had *presence.* And those eyes...

"The single women of Coffee Creek needn't worry," she assured Laurel. "I'm not going to be any competition where Dan Farley is concerned."

She was out the door before Laurel had time for a comeback. Not that it mattered. She was so *not* going to tell Laurel about the history between her and Farley. She'd never told *anyone* and she'd bet Farley hadn't, either.

Chapter Two

Dan Farley settled his coffee cup into the holder of his truck, then wolfed down the cinnamon bun in two minutes flat. Sweet and spicy…just like Cassidy Lambert.

The little witch.

So she was back in town. Judging from all the baggage in her truck, she was done with school. Would she be staying in Coffee Creek? Or moving on? Corb had mentioned she was studying accounting and thinking of working in Billings, but that her mother had other plans.

He didn't really care how it panned out. The little minx was trouble. And he intended to keep his distance.

For the longest time she'd been nothing but the cute younger sister of his best friends B.J., Corb and Brock. With no siblings of his own, he hadn't really minded when she tried to tag along with them—but Brock was always looking for ways to get rid of her.

He said she talked too much. Which was true.

He complained that she tried to boss them around. Also true.

But she had redeeming characteristics, among them a soft, yet courageous heart. So many times she'd come to him and her brothers expecting them to help a baby chick that had fallen from its nest, a fawn struggling with a lame leg, a farm cat with distemper, eyes weeping from disease, matted fur over a scrawny body.

Brock and Corb would brush her off, but he'd always done what he could to save the animal.

And then Cassidy turned twenty-one and the person who needed saving was himself. . . .

An incoming call prevented him from dredging up further unwanted memories. He pressed the button on his steering wheel to patch it through.

"Hello?"

"Farley?" It was Liz Moffat, his right-hand woman at the office. Besides being his receptionist, the thirty-three-year-old mother of four also did a pretty good job of running his private life, as well. "I just had a call from Maddie Turner."

"I'm on my way to Coffee Creek Ranch right now." The Lamberts' place was only fifteen miles from Silver Creek Ranch. Maddie Turner and Olive Lambert were sisters, though they hadn't spoken to one another in over thirty years.

"When you're finished there, could you swing by Maddie's place? One of her cows is having a difficult birth."

"I'll do that."

"Oh, and Amber wants to know about tonight. If you think you'll be able to make it in time for a movie."

He wanted to say yes, but knew better. "Tell her probably not. I still have to check out the Harringtons' lame cow."

"Maybe things will go well at Maddie's and you'll be able to do both." Liz had fixed him up with Amber and was lobbying hard for the relationship to work.

"Maybe." But he doubted it. Maddie Turner didn't have the head for business that her older sister did, and she'd been struggling financially for the past five years. She wouldn't be asking for his help if the situation with her cow and unborn calf wasn't dire.

But first he had the situation at the Lamberts' to deal with. *And maybe another chance to see Cassidy?*

No. If she knew he was there, she'd avoid the barns, the way she usually did.

CASSIDY WAS DRIVING about ten miles over the posted speed limit on the secondary road out of Coffee Creek. Plus, she was taking sips of her coffee. And nibbling on her cinnamon bun. So she couldn't claim to be the injured party when she saw the flashing lights of a patrol car behind her five minutes after leaving town.

She pulled to the side of the road, turned off her music and waited.

Sun beat in warmly through the windshield and she could hear a meadowlark's song drifting on the fragrant spring breeze that wafted through her open windows. Ahead of her the pavement curved and she tensed as she saw the flower wreath affixed to the simple white cross that marked the spot of the accident where Brock had died last July.

She'd been so busy thinking about Farley—and feeling unjustly hurt at his obvious disdain for her—that she'd almost passed right by the scene of Brock's accident without noticing.

In her rearview mirror, she saw an officer step out of the patrol car. Her nervousness increased when she recognized Savannah Moody.

The last time she'd seen Savannah had been at Brock's funeral. Savannah hadn't stayed long, but she'd paid her respects. Now Cassidy took a deep breath as the sheriff stooped so she could look in the open window.

"Hey, Cassidy. On your way home from Bozie?" Savannah wore her long hair in a braid when she was on duty, but even without her thick chestnut hair framing her face, she was stunning. She'd been blessed with large, thickly lashed eyes and smooth olive skin that she'd inherited from her French Canadian mother.

"Yes. Just finished my exams yesterday."

"I'm sure you're anxious to get home, but slow down, okay? I'm not giving you a ticket this time. Just a friendly warning."

Her gaze shifted up the road a bit, and Cassidy knew what she was thinking. Knew, too, that the warning shouldn't have been necessary.

"You're right. I'll be a lot more careful in the future." She studied the wreath again, noting that the flowers appeared fresh. "Is Maddie Turner still tending that?"

Maddie was her mother's estranged sister. No one in the family knew the whole story behind the family feud, but they'd all grown up understanding that their mother would consider it a grand betrayal if they acknowledged their aunt by so much as a smile or a word of hello.

By the same token, none of them had understood why Maddie was being so diligent in tending Brock's memorial tribute, until Corb took it upon himself to drive up to Silver Creek Ranch and ask her.

Apparently Brock had been in the habit of visiting their aunt every now and then and had even helped her out with some handyman work on occasion.

No one knew why he'd done this. But if any one of the Lambert kids was wont to break their parents' rules, Brock was definitely the one.

"I guess so." Savannah patted the side of her truck. "I'm not a fan of roadside memorials, myself. Anything that draws your eyes off the road is a potential hazard."

"I'll be careful," Cassidy promised again.

"Good. Say hi to your mom for me, Cassidy. And welcome home."

She was gone before Cassidy could tell her that this wasn't a true homecoming. She was just going to stay a few weeks until she found out about the job she'd applied for in Billings. Her first interview had gone well. Now she was hoping for a second, soon to be followed by an offer of employment.

Josh had applied to the same accounting firm, and he felt they both stood a good chance of being hired since their marks leading up to finals had been the top of their class. Competition was tight, though, since the accounting firm was only looking for three new articling students, and at least five other members of their graduating class had applied, including the woman who'd been president of the business club.

Cassidy checked for traffic—and signs of wildlife—before pulling back onto the road. Savannah was long gone, having made a U-turn and driven off in the opposite direction. Meanwhile, Cassidy continued toward home, driving a sedate five miles per hour under the limit until she came to the fork in the road where she slowed down even further.

To the right lay Silver Creek Ranch, where Maddie still lived on the Turners' homestead property.

The road to the left led to Coffee Creek Ranch, which had been in the Lambert family just as long as the Turners had owned theirs. Cassidy's father had passed away years ago, and ever since then her mother, Olive, had been running the ranch—with the help of her youngest sons and Jackson. Her mother had a good head for business, and despite some ups and downs in the cattle business, she'd done very well.

One of her strategies to combat the uncertain economic times had been to diversify into breeding American quarter horses. Now the horse breeding side of their business was bringing in as much revenue as the cattle. And even more profit, according to Jackson, who was in charge of the books.

Now that she had her business degree, Cassidy suspected her mother was going to pressure her to take over the administrative side of the ranch from Jackson. She'd made it clear that she hoped Cassidy would move back home after graduation and join in the family ranching business.

But that wasn't going to happen. Cassidy loved her mother, but it was the sort of love that did best when there were at least a hundred miles between them. And much as she loved the ranch, she thought a business career could be exciting, too. She could hardly wait to get started.

Cassidy's tires rumbled as she drove over the cattle guard that was meant to keep Coffee Creek cattle from roaming beyond their property line. A hundred yards farther down the road, she came to the small wooden bridge that crossed over one of several unnamed creeks that ran through their property.

She drove up the final hill, then paused, looking down on the homestead that had been in her father's side of the family since the mid-eighteen-hundreds. It was hard not to feel a sense of pride. From here she could see the white barns with their green roofs, stacks of rolled hay, sorting pens and chutes, and the neatly fenced paddocks and larger pastures. All the outbuildings had been constructed in the hollow of a wide valley, high enough that there would be no danger of flooding in the spring, but protected from the worst of the winds that came off the mountains.

The main house sat above the other buildings, backing onto a grove of pines and with a view out to Square Butte—a flat-topped mountain that dominated the skyline to the north.

Through a stand of ponderosa pines to her left, Cassidy could see glimmers of Cold Coffee Lake around which their father had built homes for all three of his sons.

Driving past the graveled turnoff to the lake and the cabins, Cassidy crossed through the main gate, with the wrought iron detailing of the double *C*s that were the family brand. Her tires rumbled yet again on another cattle guard. And then she was home.

Four other vehicles were already parked in the yard. Her mother's white SUV, Jackson's black one, Corb's Jeep and, of course, Farley's charcoal-and-silver truck, with the Farley & Sons logo on the side.

Cassidy slid in next to her mother's SUV, where she wouldn't block any of the other vehicles. She cut off the ignition and waited to see if her arrival had been watched for.

Given the trouble Farley had described, she hadn't been expecting a welcoming committee. Probably everyone was down at the barn with the sick horse. But there was one faithful soul waiting to greet her.

Sky, still trim and healthy-looking despite the gray flecks in her black coat, must have been sleeping on the front porch. She was sitting now, head cocked, waiting for the cue.

She'd been trained not to go near any vehicle if there were people inside. But the moment Cassidy stepped out, she came running as fast as her old hip joints would let her.

"Hey there, Sky! Oh, it's so good to see you." Cassidy crouched by her dog, wrapping her arms around her and burrowing her face in Sky's sun-warmed coat.

Sky wriggled and grunted, panted and smiled, demonstrating in every way possible her extreme happiness at having Cassidy home again.

"Has Corb been taking good care of you? You sure look pretty." Cassidy gave her dog a lot of pats and scratches, then sat up on her haunches to look around. The place was almost eerily quiet. Not even the housekeeper, placid, middle-aged Bonny, was here. Must be one of her days off.

They'd had many housekeepers over the years. Olive had exacting standards and most didn't last more than six months or so. But Bonny was made of stern stuff and had been here almost four years now. Cassidy was glad. Besides having loads of common sense—that helped her deal with Olive—she was also an excellent cook.

Cassidy patted Sky again, wondering why her dog wasn't up at Corb and Laurel's cabin. When Cassidy had left for college five years ago, she'd been living in residence and unable to bring her dog with her. Poor, lonely Sky had turned to Brock for companionship, then after his death, to Corb.

Now she lived almost full-time with Corb, Laurel and Stephanie…and yet somehow she'd known to wait at the main house today. Possibly Sky had heard Cassidy's name spoken more often than usual and had guessed she was coming home?

Cassidy didn't put it past her. Sky was a remarkable dog. When she was younger, she'd been as useful as an extra hand at moving and herding cattle. Now she was too old to work, but she was as smart as ever.

Finally, Cassidy stood, brushing the fine gravel from her knees. She could go into the house and wait for the rest of them to join her. But she'd seen Farley at the café and the world hadn't fallen apart. Besides, she was anxious to find out if Lucy was going to be okay.

She gave the signal for Sky to follow. "Come on, girl. Let's head down to the barn and find out what's going on."

WHEN HER MOTHER decided to go into the quarter horse breeding business, they'd built a new equine barn equipped to accommodate twenty to twenty-five broodmares with a separate wing for the stallions. The family's riding horses were pastured and boarded in a smaller, less high-tech barn, closer to the house. This barn—they called it the home barn—had also been updated at that time, including the addition of a new tack room and office, both of which Jackson had designed.

It was to the home barn that Cassidy headed now, Sky heeling obediently on her left. She was glad she didn't need to waste any time changing. Even when going to school in the city, she'd continued to dress the way she always had: in jeans and cowboy boots. She'd grown up in Western wear, and that was how she felt most comfortable.

In fact, her main concern about going to work for an accounting firm in the city was adjusting to the suits and high-heeled pumps she knew she'd be expected to wear. She'd bought such an outfit for job interviews and so far every time she'd worn it, she'd ended up with blisters on her heels.

Voices became audible as she drew nearer to the

barn. The main door was open and her mother, Corb and Jackson were watching while Farley examined the golden palomino in the first stall. Cassidy stopped in the doorway, as yet unnoticed, waiting to see what would happen.

Her mother looked trim in jeans and a pressed gingham shirt. No doubt hard work and a healthy diet had helped preserve her petite figure, but her silver-blond hair, styled in an attractive bob, was the result of regular monthly trips to the salon.

She had her hands on her slender hips as she watched over Lucky Lucy's examination, offering Farley pointers as he worked, which were no doubt exasperating to the experienced vet.

"Be careful," Olive said. "You don't want to hurt her."

No response from Farley.

"See how she's holding her head?" Olive continued. "Low and extended? That's not usual for her."

Farley, who would not have needed to have this pointed out, replied calmly, "She's probably doing that to relieve the pain in her throat and lymph nodes."

Of the four of them, he was the only one Cassidy couldn't see clearly because he was in the stall with the horse. Just the sound of his voice, however, made her feel nervous and excited, the same odd cocktail of emotions she'd experienced earlier in the café.

"You seen any other cases of strangles lately?" Corb asked. Her brother's shoulders were hunched with worry, as were Jackson's. Both men had their backs to her, until Sky came up between them.

"Hey there, girl." Corb bent to pat the border collie's head. "What are you doing out here? You're supposed to be on the porch, enjoying your retirement."

With that, blond, green-eyed Corb looked back toward the house, and a smile slowly broke through his serious expression.

"Look who's home. How're you doing, Cass?"

Of all her family, Corb was Cassidy's favorite. He was easygoing, like their father had been, with a warm smile and eyes that sparkled with good humor. With his blond hair and green eyes, he was also the brother that looked most like her. If they'd been closer in age, people probably would have taken them for twins.

He gave her a one-armed hug, pulling her up between him and Jackson.

Her foster brother had dark, brooding good looks, and a natural reserve that made him difficult to really know. But the smile he gave her now was kind and friendly. "Hey, Cassidy, good to see you."

"You, too, Jackson." She felt her throat tighten. "Hi, Mom."

"Sweetheart." Olive swooped in and gave Cassidy a hug and a kiss. "How were your exams?" Then, Olive continued without waiting for an answer, "I was saddling Lucky Lucy for a ride this morning when I spotted some nasal discharge. I don't blame Jackson for not noticing sooner, even though the horses are now his responsibility."

"Jackson has a lot on his hands these days besides overseeing the care of the home horses," Corb said mildly, countering his mother's implied criticism. "Spring is the busiest time of year for all of us and he's had four new foals birthed this week alone. Plus he's busy with the mare breeding program for the quarter horses."

Cassidy admired the way Corb managed to stand up to their mother without getting upset. All her brothers—except maybe B.J.—were better at that skill than she was.

Every time she came home, she did so with the resolve that *this time* would be different. She wouldn't let her mother get to her. She wouldn't lose her cool. But neither would she let her mother derail her. She had her own plans for her own life. And that was that.

"My exams went well, Mom, but I'm sorry about Lucky Lucy. Is it strangles for sure?" She moved in closer and Farley, who'd been collecting a sample of mucus, now sealed the cotton swab into a vial.

Then he straightened. For the second time that day he took her measure.

"I'm pretty sure. She's got some swelling around the jaw area, as well as a fever and clear nasal discharge."

Cassidy shifted her gaze from the vet to the horse. Lucy was gorgeous, and as recently as her last visit home for Stephanie's baby shower, had been very healthy. She patted Lucy's flank, then moved in closer.

"Remember me, sweet thing?" she murmured. "We had a great ride together last February. 'Course there was some snow we had to contend with back then."

As if in answer, Lucy coughed, and more discharge gathered in her nasal cavity. Cassidy glanced at Farley, hoping for reassurance. "How bad is it? Is she suffering?"

"Feel here." Farley took her hand and guided it to a swollen area on Lucy's neck. "Her lymph nodes are pretty enlarged. I'm sure it's causing her pain or she wouldn't be distending her neck like this."

"Oh, you poor thing." Cassidy gentled her with soft strokes, trying to erase the feeling of Farley's strong, capable hands over hers. Lucy nickered, voicing her appreciation of the extra attention.

"I'll run a test just to be sure," Farley said. "But for now we'd better assume that she does have strangles."

"Crap." Jackson sounded disgusted. "We'll have to disinfect everything, won't we?"

"Afraid so." Farley kept a hand on Lucky Lucy as he walked around her, then out to the aisle. "Good thing you keep your riding horses separate from the breeders. Hopefully the quarter horses will be fine. But I'd recommend no sales or purchases until the strangles is under control."

Olive made an impatient sound. "Is that really necessary? You said yourself, we have the two operations completely separate."

"Just to be sure, I think it is. You'll have to set up a quarantine area here in the barn. Watch the other horses carefully. Any of them show signs of the disease, then they'll need to be separated, too."

Jackson rubbed his unshaven chin. "This is going to mean a lot of extra work. Frankly me and my men are stretched to our limits right now…and Corb and his wranglers are, too."

"Jackson's right about that," Corb was quick to agree. "Most of the calves have been born, but we've got branding and vaccinating…and soon we'll need to be moving the herd to higher ground."

Suddenly it seemed like everyone was looking at Cassidy. *Heck and darn.* "You know I'm only home for a couple of weeks, right?"

Olive frowned at that, but Corb wasn't deterred.

"A couple of weeks could see us through the worst of this. If we're lucky." He turned to Farley. "What's involved, exactly?"

Farley shook his head. "Strangles is incredibly contagious. It can be passed on through indirect contact with buckets, feed, grass, fences and especially water troughs."

"I don't see why our quarter horses should be under quarantine then," Olive said sharply. "We feed, water and pasture them entirely separately from the riding horses."

"The infection can also be transmitted by flies," Jackson replied calmly. "Still, I have to wonder how Lucy caught this. I haven't heard of any other cases in the area."

"Have you brought any new horses onto the property lately?" Farley placed the vial for testing into his black case, then went to the sink at the corner of the barn and washed his hands.

Jackson shook his head no, then glanced at Olive. "Didn't I see you load Lucy in the trailer last week?"

"That wasn't Lucy," Olive said shortly. "I *did* buy some secondhand tack at auction on the weekend."

"That could be your culprit. I hate to say it, but your whole tack room should be disinfected. You're going to need to stock up on chlorhexidine soap."

"We have some," Corb said, pointing to a gallon by the sink.

"You're going to need more. But I have a few gallons in my truck I can give you for now." He turned to Cassidy. "If you're in charge of containing this infection, we should sit down somewhere and talk." He looked as excited as if he'd just sentenced himself to an hour in a dentist's chair.

Cassidy felt the same way herself. After a semester of studies, she'd hoped to spend most of her break on the back of a horse—not cooped up in a barn with a bucket and a rag.

"You two might as well talk in the office." Olive

waved to the door next to the tack room. "I'll bring out some coffee and sandwiches. I know Corb and Jackson will be happy to get back to work."

"Over the moon with excitement," Corb teased. He gave Cassidy a tap on the shoulder. "We'll catch up later, okay? Come by tonight and say hi to Laurel and Stephanie?"

"I did drop in at the café for a visit on my way through town, but I'll still take you up on that offer."

"Better disinfect your arms and hands, if you've had any contact with Lucy," Farley warned as the two men and Olive left the barn. "And your boots."

"I'll set up a boot dip right now." Cassidy found a plastic tub in the tack room and mixed up a disinfecting solution. She set the tub by the door so that anyone leaving the barn would be able to disinfect their boots on their way out.

Corb, Jackson and her mother all made use of the new boot dip then headed off to their respective chores.

And then it was just the two of them in a barn that was suddenly, uncomfortably silent.

For a second Cassidy considered trying to clear the air between them. But how could she possibly do that? What she'd done had been inexcusable, even if she'd only been twenty-one at the time.

Instead, she headed for the office, trusting Farley to follow, which he did, along with Sky.

The border collie settled at her feet when she sat in the oak chair behind the desk. Farley took the upholstered chair opposite, dwarfing the thing with his tall, muscular frame.

It took a lot of physical strength to be a large-animal vet, and no one could doubt that Farley had that. But it was more than his size that she found intimidating right now. When Farley looked you in the eyes, you could tell he wasn't one to compromise.

Or make allowances.

Cassidy found paper and a pen for taking notes, then waited for her instructions. As the silence stretched on, she forced herself to meet the vet's gaze.

"What can I do to help Lucy?"

"Hot compresses on her swollen glands. The abscesses will probably rupture on their own in about a week, but if they don't, I'll need to lance them."

Cassidy made a note. *Hot compresses.* "Anything else?"

"It's important that she keep eating and drinking to maintain her strength. You can try feeding her gruel—that might go down easier than her usual hay mixture. But the majority of your effort should go into keeping the infection contained."

She nodded, well aware of the risks.

"As well as keeping Lucy quarantined from the other horses you'll need to clean and disinfect her water buckets and feed containers daily. Bedding should be burned, walls and fences scrubbed down." His gaze fell to her hands, which were smooth and pale after so many months of study. "You up for all of that?"

"Guess I'll have to be."

"There's more. Any contaminated pasture areas should be rested for at least four weeks."

"You want those scrubbed down, too?"

One corner of his mouth turned up slightly. "Fortunately for you, ultraviolet light from the sun has natural antibacterial qualities."

"Yeah. I'm feeling really lucky right now. As is Lucy, I'm sure."

Once more Farley seemed to struggle not to smile.

And seeing that, she felt an ache for the easy friendship that they'd once shared.

Though *friendship* wasn't quite the right word. She'd had a crush on him dating back to the days when he and her brothers would hang out together. As a young girl, she'd followed them around the ranch until Brock ran out of patience and came up with some devious plan to get rid of her.

"Remember the time you, Corb and Brock lured me up the hayloft in the old cattle barn, then pulled down the ladder and stranded me up there?"

Farley blinked. She'd disarmed him by bringing up a story from so long ago, before the trouble between them.

"I do. How did you get down, by the way?"

"One of the hired hands heard me yelling and came to the rescue."

"You were quite the tomboy back then. But I guess it's going to be accounting offices and city life for you now, huh?"

"You say that like it's a bad thing."

He shrugged. "I'm not the only one who's surprised."

This was true. Corb, B.J. and her mother had all tried to talk her out of studying business when she'd first told them about her plans to go to college. She didn't know if they didn't think she was smart enough, or what, but they certainly hadn't been supportive.

"Yoo-hoo," her mother's voice rang out. A few seconds later she breezed in the door with a tray. "I don't mean to interrupt, just wanted to bring you some lunch."

She'd brought out a carafe of coffee with mugs and a plate of sandwiches. After setting the tray on the middle of the desk between them, she stood back and looked from Cassidy to Farley with a smile of satisfaction.

"Actually," Farley said, "we were just finishing up here."

"Don't be in such a rush. You have to eat, don't you? Take your time. I'm sure you two have a lot of catching up to do."

And with that, Olive left, making a point of closing the door behind her.

Olive didn't often make herself scarce, so Cassidy couldn't help but be suspicious. Was it possible her mother was hoping she and Farley…?

No. It couldn't be.

She risked a quick look at the vet's expression, trying to judge if he'd felt any weird vibes from her mother, too.

"Olive seems to be in a good mood for a rancher who has just had her livestock quarantined," he commented, reaching for one of the ham-and-cheese triangles.

"Yeah. She's up to something." She felt the hot color rising on her neck.

"Matchmaking?" Farley suggested.

"Kind of looks that way, doesn't it?"

"A little," he admitted. The light in his eyes grew darker, colder. "Guess you forgot to tell her that I'm the last man on earth you'd ever want to be with."

Chapter Three

It wasn't true. Farley *wasn't* the last man on earth she'd
want to be with. But she *had* told him he was. One minute before leaving the dance she'd gone to as his date—
on the arm of another man.

At least, she'd *tried* to leave with another guy. Oddly
enough, she couldn't remember the name of that other
guy anymore. But she did recall that *she'd* been the
one to ask *him* to dance. With Farley on the sidelines,
silent and angry, they'd danced an entire set together
before she'd convinced the other guy that he wanted to
drive her home.

They'd left the dance floor arm in arm. But Farley,
in a voice that was not open to negotiation, had stepped
in at that point. "You came to the dance with me. I'm
damn well seeing you home safely."

The other guy had stepped aside hastily then, no
doubt having assessed Farley's size and the girth of his
biceps, and decided he liked the current shape of his
nose just fine, thank you very much.

Cassidy had endured a fifteen-minute drive in Farley's truck during which time not a single word was
spoken. When they'd pulled up to the ranch house, he'd
been out of the truck so fast that he had her door open
before she'd even located the lever to do it herself. With

his arms crossed over his broad chest, he'd stood watching until she was safely inside her home. Only then had he driven away.

And he'd pretty much never spoken to her since then. Did she blame him? No.

Was she embarrassed for the way she'd acted? Hell, yes.

The truth was, she never should have accepted his invitation to the dance in the first place. But he'd caught her off guard in the Lonesome Spur Bar on the night of her twenty-first birthday. She'd been out having her first legal drink with a group of friends when he caught her eye and crossed the room.

She'd been ridiculously excited. Farley was older, hot and sooo handsome. And suddenly he had noticed her, too.

"Is it true?" he'd asked her, dark eyes smoldering with an emotion she'd never seen in them before. "Pretty Cassidy Lambert is no longer jailbait?"

"I stopped being jailbait a long time ago," she'd announced with a voice full of sass and vinegar. That didn't mean she wasn't quaking inside. She'd assumed Farley was completely out of her league. But now he was finally seeing her as someone other than his friends' annoying little sister.

He'd asked her to the Harvest Dance being held in the community hall the next evening. She'd accepted. And then all it had taken was one dance in his arms and she'd panicked.

Simple as that.

"Is it too late for me to apologize for my behavior that night? I was just a kid."

"No." Farley placed a hand on the desk. "If you'd still been a kid, I wouldn't have gone near you."

"I suppose that's true. But I was young."

"It wasn't the classiest move I've ever seen, Cass. But it was honest. You always were one for knowing what you wanted." He paused, then added pointedly, "And what you didn't."

She stared at him mutely. How could he talk as if he knew her so well, when she, herself, had never quite figured out why she'd acted the way she had that night? She hadn't been then, and wasn't now, a man-crazy sort of woman who liked to go on lots of dates and play one guy off another.

"I should get going. I've got another call to make before I head back to my office. You're clear on how to handle the strangles?"

She nodded, not bothering to point out that he'd only eaten one of her mother's sandwiches. She guessed that her company wasn't conducive to a good appetite on his part. She'd been so wrong to think that talking about that night would clear the air between them or ease her guilty conscience.

If anything, she felt worse.

It wasn't the classiest move I've ever seen, Cass.

God, she felt about four inches high right now.

Clumsily she got to her feet, almost knocking over her mug of coffee as she moved out from behind the desk.

Farley's eyes stayed cool. "I can see myself out."

"I know." She followed him, anyway. "But I just wanted to ask you about something else."

"What is it?"

"You said I should watch the rest of the horses in case they get sick, too. But what, exactly, should I be looking for?"

"Glad you asked that." Farley opened the office door, waited for her to pass through, then exited himself. "Don't wait until you see nasal discharge or hear the horse coughing. If any of your horses go off their feed, or seem to lack their usual energy, separate them from the rest of the herd immediately and give me a call."

"Okay." They both washed up at the sink again and used the boot dip before leaving the barn.

Midafternoon sun had Cassidy wishing she had the sunglasses she'd left behind in her truck. Squinting, she glanced at Farley, who was setting a quick pace toward his own vehicle.

"How long will we be under quarantine?"

Farley tossed his black case into the passenger side of the truck. He paused a moment to consider her question. "*If* you're diligent with disinfecting, *if* Lucy recovers quickly and *if* none of the other horses come down with it, I'd say about three weeks."

"That's a long time."

"Yeah, but better to contain this thing now before it spreads and becomes a bigger problem." He narrowed his eyes. "Or were you not planning to stay in Coffee Creek that long?"

"That depends on whether I get a job offer or not."

"You excited about spending your life as a pencil pusher in a city high-rise?"

"Why not?" she countered, placing her hands on her hips and narrowing her gaze. "You think swabbing mucus from a sick horse's nostril is so much better?"

"Actually, I do." He reached for his hat, settling it on his head, before giving her a final, parting nod. "But I wouldn't expect you to understand why. Though the little girl who grew up on this ranch would get it."

"TAKE A LOOK at these paint chips, sweetie," Olive said. "Which one do you like better with these fabric samples for your new duvet cover?"

Cassidy had just hauled her suitcase into her old bedroom, halting when she saw her mother sitting amid piles of fabric swatches and paint chips spread over the blue-and-white quilt she'd had as long as she could remember.

The handmade quilt was an heirloom from her grandmother Lambert. Cassidy had always loved it, though admittedly the fabric was now threadbare on the edges.

"What's this about, Mother?" She was tired after the long drive and the stressful encounter with Farley. Bad enough that they had strangles on the ranch and that she was in charge of containing it. If only her mother could have called some other vet rather than Farley.

"We haven't decorated your room since you were a little girl. Don't you think it's time to spruce it up a little? I thought we'd paint and order new curtains and bedding. That desk in the corner is too small for you now. What do you say about replacing it with an armoire? A beautiful antique would look lovely in that corner. I saw one in Lewistown the other day that would be perfect."

Since the bed was unavailable, Cassidy hoisted her heavy suitcase up on the desk that her mother had just pointed out. "What's the point in fixing up the room when I'm only here for a few weeks?"

"That's if you get the job," Olive reminded her. "It's always good to have a backup plan and you know you always have a home and a job here with us."

"Mom, I've told you that isn't what I want to do with

my life. If I don't end up getting this job, I'll apply for another."

"So you really mean to follow in B.J.'s footsteps, do you?" Her mother did nothing to hide her disappointment.

B.J. had been traveling the rodeo circuit for almost as long as Cassidy could remember. He'd left home at eighteen and though he made the occasional pit stop at home, he never stayed long.

"I'm not planning to start competing in rodeos, Mom."

"That's not what I meant and you know it. This land has been in our family for five generations. Your father and I planned things so we have room enough and work enough for all of you."

Then why didn't Dad build me one of those cottages he had made for the boys?

Cassidy didn't voice the question, even though it was often on her mind. The truth was, she'd never wanted to live so close to her mother. Nevertheless, it did rankle that she'd never even been offered what had been so freely given to her brothers.

"Mom, you just finished helping me get five years of higher education. Surely you must want me to put it to good use."

"You could take over the bookkeeping and taxes here at our ranch. Handle our dealings with the bank and manage our investments."

And be under the thumb of her mother and brothers for the rest of her life? "Mom, I have to make my own way. Do my own thing."

"You think you'll be happy living in Billings for the rest of your life?"

"It's not that far. I'll visit. Like I did when I was going to school in Bozeman."

Her mom pressed a hand to her forehead. "That is not the right plan for you. I promise you, Cassie, you'll be making a big mistake if you walk away from your heritage."

Stay calm. Stay firm. That was Cassidy's new mantra and she was determined to stick to it. "It's my life, Mom. And my decision."

Olive sighed. She turned her gaze to the view out the window, then back to Cassidy. "Let's drop it for now. I don't want a big argument to spoil your first day home."

Right. 'Cause it had been such a great day so far.

Cassidy took a deep breath and reminded herself that she'd vowed to try harder with her mother. "Why don't we go to the kitchen, brew a pot of tea and talk about something else?"

"In a minute." Olive picked up two paint squares. "I promised Abby at the hardware store I'd phone and place my order this afternoon. Which do you prefer? The sage-green or the buttercream?"

DAN FARLEY DROVE away from Coffee Creek Ranch feeling disappointed, unsettled…frustrated. He wasn't usually a man given to complicated emotions. What was it about Cassidy Lambert? After all these years she ought to be nothing to him.

But it didn't help that she'd shown such concern for the sick horse. He'd always been a sucker for her soft heart.

And it helped even less that she still filled out her jeans in all the right places. Add in that beautiful blond hair and those disarming green eyes—hell, any man could be excused for losing his head over a girl like Cassidy.

But he didn't want to do it twice.

To distract himself, he decided to check in with Liz.

"Just finished at the Lamberts' and I'm on my way to Silver Creek."

"That took a while."

Liz was probably worried he wouldn't make the date with Amber. Why did all women assume a man wasn't happy unless he was suitably married?

"Yeah. I've put the place under quarantine. We'll have to run the tests, but I'm pretty sure about the result."

"Bad luck for them," Liz allowed. "Good luck at Silver Creek. Hopefully things will go better there."

MADDIE TURNER WAS waiting for him when he arrived, a stocky woman with wiry gray hair and plain features—quite the contrast to her fine-featured, well-coiffed sister, Olive. The two border collies flanking her were younger versions of Cassidy's dog, Sky. The dogs looked anxious, just like their owner.

Maddie was wearing faded overalls and a threadbare shirt—both smeared with blood. Her face was damp and she appeared exhausted. He knew from experience that helping a cow with a difficult delivery was hard, physical labor.

"You okay?"

"Been better. Thanks for getting here so fast," she said, as he grabbed his gear out of the truck, then slipped on a pair of overalls.

"I was next door at Coffee Creek."

She didn't blink an eye at the mention of her sister's

place. "Lucky you were so close. I don't think we have much time."

She led the way to the barn, where he could hear the sounds of distress from the mother-to-be. They found the poor thing on the stall floor, with terror in her wide brown eyes.

She looked on the small side. Young. "This her first calf?"

Maddie nodded.

A quick exam confirmed that the calf was positioned backward and upside down. A C-section was their only hope. "Anyone else around?" he asked hopefully.

"Nope."

"No hired help?"

She avoided eye contact. "I've had to cut back lately."

"Too bad. We could use an extra set of hands here." Or two, or four. He started setting out his equipment, going through the steps in his head. Since he didn't have an assistant, he needed to have everything at the ready before he prepped the cow for the incision.

"I can secure her head," Maddie offered.

He wasn't so sure about that. Maddie looked pretty exhausted. "How long has she been in labor?"

"I brought her in from the field a few days ago. Just had a feeling she was going to have some trouble. Sure enough when I came out this morning I could see that her labor had started, but wasn't going anywhere."

He sighed. "Okay. We better not lose any more time."

"I agree." Maddie moved behind the prone cow, sinking to the straw bedding and then locking the animal's head to prevent her from moving around. The exhausted heifer didn't even resist.

"Poor thing," Maddie said softly. "Don't you worry. Doc Farley is going to get this critter out of you."

The tender caring in Maddie Turner's voice and the firm yet gentle way she handled the animal reminded Farley of her niece, Cassidy, trying to comfort Lucky Lucy earlier.

He shelved the thought, returning his focus to the job at hand. Maddie couldn't afford to lose the calf or the cow. More than money was at stake here, though, and Farley was determined not to fail.

AN HOUR AND a half later, the new mother and her matching black calf were resting in the barn, and Farley and Maddie were in the kitchen having coffee. Farley was tired, but pleased. Helping to bring new life into the world was one of the most rewarding aspects of his job.

He ought to be on the road, heading to the next ranch. But he sensed Maddie wasn't ready to be alone, so he'd agreed to stop in for a bit. Now Maddie placed a plate with crackers and cheese on the table.

"Sorry I don't have anything more substantial to offer. You must be starving. I know I am." She opened the upper freezer compartment of her fridge. "I could fry up some sausage and eggs if you have twenty minutes to spare."

He thought about the lame cow and the forty-five minutes it would take to drive to the Harringtons' spread. Then he thought about Amber and the movie she'd been hoping to see. That was out of the question now. But hopefully he could still manage a late dinner. "I really don't."

"Didn't think so." Maddie closed the fridge door, then sank into a chair and reached for her coffee. Her dogs were in the room with them. Farley thought he had them straight now. Trix was sleeping on the mat by the back door and Honey was curled up under the table. As well as the dogs, there was a cat prowling the place, too. Short-haired and ginger-colored, she'd slunk into the room earlier, taken Farley's measure, then exited with nose held high.

Maddie's kitchen was a warm, cozy place. The wooden table and chairs had the sort of "distressed" look that came from decades of being used and not coddled, as did the wooden floors and cabinets. The counters were cluttered, but clean, and the big farm sink gleamed as if it had been disinfected recently.

The focal point of the room was the antique, black, wood-burning cookstove. Warm air drifted from the stove to soothe the sore muscles of Farley's shoulders and upper back. He fought the urge to close his eyes, knowing that if he succumbed to sleep he might find himself still in this room an hour later.

He crunched down on a couple of crackers and a slab of the cheddar, then followed the food with a swallow of hot, almost scalding, coffee. Maddie made it the old-fashioned way, boiled in a percolator on the stove.

"So what's up at Coffee Creek?" Maddie asked him.

He hesitated before answering. Everyone in the community of Coffee Creek was aware of the rift between the Turner sisters, though no one knew the exact cause. Some people felt that Olive's marriage to neighboring rancher Bobby Lambert had been the start of it. One fact was irrefutable: Maddie hadn't attended their wedding. And despite the size of the wedding—apparently several hundred—the absence had been very conspicuous.

"One of their horses has strangles," he finally said.

"Sorry to hear that." Maddie sounded genuinely concerned.

"Hopefully it hasn't had time to spread. They have

the sick horse quarantined and Cassidy is going to be disinfecting the barn."

"Cassidy? So she's home from college, is she?"

Maddie seemed to know a lot about her sister's family. He supposed he shouldn't be surprised. Since she'd never married herself or had children, the Lamberts were her closest relations. Which only made the feud between the sisters that much sadder.

"Only for a few weeks, apparently. She's hoping to get a job with some accounting firm in Billings."

"Really? I can't imagine Olive letting her do that."

"I'm not sure Olive has much say in the matter."

Maddie's lips tightened. "Then you don't know my sister very well."

"She hasn't been able to keep B.J. from the rodeo circuit," he pointed out.

"All the more reason she's going to fight like hell to keep her daughter close to home."

"You think? Cassidy's no pushover." Tenacity was in her DNA. And growing up with all those brothers had only made her tougher and more resilient.

"You don't know Olive," Maddie repeated.

"Not as well as you do, obviously," he allowed. "But my money's still on Cassidy."

Chapter Four

Cassidy took the time to have tea with her mother, then changed into rubber boots and gloves and headed back to the barn. She had her faults, but avoiding hard work wasn't one of them.

After diluting the disinfectant that Farley had left with her, she started with the horse troughs and feeding buckets. Once those had been thoroughly washed and rinsed, she went to check on Lucy.

Oh, how she hated to see the sweet mare in obvious discomfort. Lucy had a fierce spirit, but she was also gentle and trusting with her rider. Olive had purchased her from one of the best trainers in Montana and it showed. Cassidy had known she'd spent a pretty penny on her, too, when Olive demurred from sharing the purchase price with them.

Privately, Cassidy thought Lucy's potential was being wasted as a working horse on a cattle ranch. She had lovely footing. Cassidy bet she'd make a great barrel-racing horse. And she was so pretty, she'd be a real crowd favorite.

In high school Cassidy had dabbled in the sport, coached by her brothers and encouraged by her mom. But in her final school year she'd decided she needed to focus on her grades and she'd given up competing.

She hadn't run a course since.

"Hey, Lucy. Think you'd like being the center of attention in a rodeo ring?"

The worst waste of all, of course, would be if Lucy didn't recover from the strangles. Cassidy took some comfort from the fact that Farley hadn't seemed overly worried.

Cassidy went to the tack room to heat some compresses, then returned to Lucy's stall.

"I have something here that should help you feel better."

Lucy nickered and shuffled restlessly. Her nostrils were oozing pus again and she looked as miserable as a horse could look without actually collapsing to the ground.

Cassidy pressed the heated pads against the mare's swollen lymph nodes. "How does that feel?" She'd wash down the stalls next, then mix up some warm mash for Lucy. She had fencing to clean and the tack room, too, but that might have to wait for tomorrow because she needed to examine the rest of the riding horses before nightfall and make sure none of them were exhibiting signs of the sickness.

Three hours later, Cassidy finally made it back to the ranch house, where she showered and had dinner with her mother. Olive was hurrying the meal because she had a meeting in town at seven.

"I'm sorry to rush out on your first night home. But if I don't go they'll just make a bunch of silly decisions that I'll have to fix the next meeting."

The committee was working to build a historical site at the intersection of Highway 81 and Main Street, kitty-corner to the Crossroads Gas and Snack. A life-sized bronze of a quarter horse had been donated to the town and the idea was to have a walking loop around the statue with wooden signposts detailing the history of the area.

Olive had been shepherding the project from the start and had contributed a significant chunk of cash to the fundraising efforts.

"That's fine, Mom. I'll run over and visit Corb and the gang."

"I hate to leave you with the dishes…"

"Not a problem. Have fun at your meeting."

Her mom grabbed her leather coat from the closet at the side door, then slipped on her best pair of go-to-meeting boots. "If you think fun is even a possibility, then you haven't met Straws Monahan."

Cassidy chuckled at that, knowing that even the strong-minded Straws whose property was on the other side of Coffee Creek, closer to Lewistown, would be no match for her mother.

Fifteen minutes later, the kitchen was spotless and Cassidy slipped outside to walk to her brother's. Sky followed at her side for the quarter of a mile to Cold Coffee Lake Road. Trees—a mixture of aspen and ponderosa pine—separated each of the brothers' cabins, giving them some privacy from one another.

Jackson lived in the cabin closest to the main house. Originally built for B.J., when it had become clear that he was going to be on the road most of the time, Olive had reluctantly given permission for Jackson to take up residence.

The other cabin had been Brock's. It was vacant now, and Cassidy had no idea what would become of it. She'd heard Corb suggest that Olive offer it to Winnie, but that idea had gone over like a lead balloon.

Olive and Winnie had been like oil and water from

the start. Cassidy knew, since her mother had confided in her, that Olive had hoped Brock would marry someone else. And that she felt Winnie fell short of the mark as far as being the wife of a cattleman.

Cassidy hadn't bothered arguing.

Nothing she said had ever changed her mother's opinion on anything, anyway.

Cassidy helped Sky up the stairs to Corb and Laurel's front door. Exhausted from the walk, Sky seemed happy to curl up on a plump cushion on the plank floor of the porch that was obviously a favorite sleeping spot.

Since the door had been left open a crack, Cassidy gave it a nudge. "Hello?"

"Come on in!" It was Laurel who answered. "We were hoping you'd drop by."

Cassidy left her boots in the foyer and found Laurel in the kitchen, where the counters were littered with stacked dishes and pots and pans.

Laurel didn't seem perturbed by the mess. She was at the sink, her hands in soapy water. "Hey, Cassidy, some homecoming. I hear you spent the day disinfecting in the barn. But I bet that wasn't as bad as this mess." She wrinkled her nose at the stove behind her.

Cassidy came round the counter to give her sister-in-law a hug. Once more she thought how smart Corb had been to marry this woman. Laurel's easygoing nature and sense of humor were a good match for him.

"Yeah, it's been a chaotic day." Cassidy glanced at the stove, which was splattered with baked-on tomato sauce and something that looked like egg yolk. "You, too?"

"Every day's chaotic when you have a new baby. After two months you'd think I'd have things fig-

ured out and be on some sort of schedule, but you'd
be wrong."

Cassidy laughed. Already she felt more relaxed than
she'd been all day. "Where's the rest of the family?"

"Corb's giving Stephanie her bath upstairs. They'll
be down in a sec." She glanced at her own T-shirt, which
had some stains matching those on the stove. "I could
use a bath myself. Not to mention some clean clothes.
Sorry to be such a slob."

"You look just fine." Cassidy picked up a towel to
dry the dishes Laurel was washing. "Babies must be
addictive. I can't wait to see the little peanut again and
kiss every inch of that adorable little face."

"Maybe I should shave first." Corb was down the
stairs, with Stephanie tucked into one arm like a foot-
ball. "Gosh, Cass, I had no idea you were so fond of
your older brother."

For answer, she snapped the towel at his back. "Hand
over that cutie-pie. Your wife needs your help in the
kitchen."

"This is so not a fair trade," Corb grumbled. But he
smiled as he handed his daughter to his sister. "Do you
think her hair is red? I think it is, but Laurel swears
it's blond."

"Maybe strawberry-blond?" Cassidy said, in compromise, though she agreed with Corb. Stephanie felt
wonderful in her arms. She'd lost the fragility of a new-
born, but was still, definitely, an infant. All soft and
sweet and cuddly, with wide green eyes that stared right
at her.

"Jeez, why wasn't I assigned child-care duty instead
of put on the quarantine detail?" Cassidy started swaying, in a way that felt instinctual.

"Wait two hours and you'll be glad you ended up

with the job you have," Laurel advised. "Stephanie is a great baby, but evening is her cranky time. She doesn't usually settle until around midnight, and then she's up like clockwork at three for another feeding."

"That sounds tough," Cassidy said with a grimace. "Still, it's great to have a baby in the family."

Corb and Laurel exchanged a glance. Then Corb said, "Actually, there are two babies in our family now."

"What?" Her brother wasn't making any sense. But Laurel knew what he was talking about. Cassidy turned to her sister-in-law. "What the heck does he mean by that?"

Laurel looked nervous. She glanced at Corb, then said, "Winnie had a baby. A little boy."

Cassidy collapsed on a handy stool. "Is it Brock's?"

Laurel nodded. "Winnie was two months pregnant on their wedding day. She hadn't told Brock yet, so he didn't know."

"Wow." Cassidy felt numb at the news. Then slowly she took in the ramifications. "Brock left behind a son." There was some comfort in that.

She did the math next.

"But if she was two months pregnant last July, then Winnie would have had her baby sometime in January."

"That's right," Laurel agreed.

"So that's the 'health issue' that's been keeping her at home with her parents?"

"Winnie almost lost the baby after Brock died. Her doctor prescribed bed rest. And calm."

"I get that she had to stay with her parents. But why didn't she tell any of us about the baby?"

"She did make a few overtures to your mother. But Olive never returned her calls. To be honest, I think

Winnie is still bitter that Olive wasn't warmer to her during the engagement period."

Cassidy couldn't fault Winnie for feeling that way. Still. "Winnie's baby is our nephew. Mom's grandchild. She should have told us."

"That's how I feel," Corb said.

"As Winnie's best friend, I've been conflicted. I promised her I would let her decide on the right time to tell your family. But obviously I had to tell Corb. And he's been patient, but—"

"Enough is enough." Corb shook his head. "Winnie's had her chance to break the news. Since she hasn't, Laurel and I have to be the ones to tell the family. You're the first one to find out. We'll tell Mom next."

"Can you do me a favor and do it when I'm not around?"

Corb laughed, then asked how things had gone in the barn. "I meant to check on Lucy after I finished my chores, but I knew Laurel couldn't wait to see me."

"More like you couldn't wait to see Laurel," Cassidy guessed, bending down to smooch the baby while her brother and his wife exchanged a kiss.

"So what was up with you and Farley earlier?" Corb asked. "God, the tension in that barn was something else. You two never had a thing, did you?"

Of course Laurel picked up on the suggestion right away. "I'll bet you anything they did. They were both in the Cinnamon Stick at the same time today," she told her husband, passing him a bowl to dry at the same time. "Wicked sparks."

Corb looked at the bowl he'd just dried as if he'd never seen it before, then shrugged and placed it on the table. "Anyway, I thought you had a boyfriend in college? Jed something or other…"

"His name is Josh. Josh Brown. And he's not really a boyfriend."

"Though he'd like to be?" Laurel guessed.

"Maybe…"

"Let's get back to Farley. Fill in the blanks, sister dear."

Cassidy had never considered her family to be an especially sensitive or perceptive bunch. So why was everyone picking up on all these vibes between her and Farley?

She had to set them straight. And now.

"Farley and I don't have a *thing*. He just doesn't like me very much. And I guess the feeling is mutual."

"He doesn't like you very much," Corb repeated, as if sounding out the words for someone with limited understanding. "Right. That's totally believable, Cass. Good cover."

He had inside information of some sort, she realized. Which could only have come from one source. "What did Farley tell you, Corb?"

Her brother just gave her an innocent grin. From experience she knew that nothing she did or said would get him to spill the beans.

Brothers.

Why couldn't her parents have given her at least *one* sister?

"AT SOME POINT you have to put your own life on your priority list, Farley."

Liz sounded more upset than Amber had when he'd called to bow out of their date. He couldn't make the movie—*or* the dinner.

Farley pulled into the lane leading to the home where he'd lived all his life—except for the years he'd spent going to university in Bozeman and Washington. The ranch house had been built on the south end of four sections of wide-open meadows with timbered ridges and a mile of Careless Creek flowing through it.

Once upon a time his ancestors had tried their hand at cattle ranching, but his grandfather and father had both abandoned those efforts in favor of veterinary practice, renting out the rest of the land to their neighbors who used some for grazing and the rest for hay.

The old barn had long since been converted into an office, with examining rooms and stalls and pens for housing animals that required overnight stays.

"The situation at the Harringtons' was serious, Liz." If only they'd called him in three weeks earlier, instead of trying to diagnose the problem themselves. "I couldn't just walk out on them to go watch a movie."

"You need to partner with another vet, Farley. There's too much work for one man alone. Frankly, you could use more office staff, as well. You may be willing to forgo a personal life, but I have four kids and a husband. I hate to leave my work undone at the end of the day, but lately I've had to do it."

"I know you work hard. And I appreciate it." No way would he put up with all these lectures she gave him if he didn't.

"Thank you. But you're missing the point. I wasn't looking for a pat on the back. It's time you made room for more in your life. To put it plainly—besides a business partner, you also need a wife."

If he was talking to anyone else, he would have hung up at this point. But Liz was right about one thing— she kept his life running as smoothly as possible and he couldn't do without her.

"I don't have time for a girlfriend, let alone a wife." He pulled up to the garage and shifted into Park.

"That's because—"

"I'm home now. Gotta go, Liz."

He turned off the ignition and the Bluetooth cut out, truncating the rest of his very capable assistant's advice. He loved Liz. Usually. And then there were times when he'd like to trade her in for a quieter model.

His dogs met him as soon as he stepped out of his SUV. Tom and Dick were mongrel terrier mixes, part of a litter dropped off at his clinic five years ago. They'd proven to be great companions, much less trouble than either a girlfriend or a wife. If only he could train them to answer phones and work the computer, he'd be set.

"Hey, guys. You hungry? I know I am." Farley made his way in through the side door into a large mudroom with a bathroom attached. He always had a shower and changed after work, no matter how tired or starving he was.

The dogs knew this and they waited patiently for him to finish.

Next on the priority list were his dogs. Not a big believer in doggy kibble, Farley fed them a special, home-made mash that he kept in the refrigerator. Both dogs loved it and went straight to their ceramic bowls by the far wall to gobble and enjoy.

Now it was his turn.

Farley surveyed his gourmet kitchen.

Five years ago when his parents retired, he'd sold one section of his land and pumped the money into the sprawling ranch house. He'd put in heated slate floors, new maple cabinetry and all the high-end appliances, as well as redoing the bathrooms. The old windows were

replaced with triple panes that blocked UV light and a
new red metal roof replaced the aging asphalt shingles.

He'd bought furniture, too, the kind you saw when
you booked into an upscale mountain resort. His house
was now his castle, in every sense of the word.

Maybe it was a little on the big side for just one man
and two dogs. But you never knew. One day another
dog might come along and join the family. As a vet, it
was bound to happen sooner or later.

Sometimes his mom got on his case, too. Like Liz,
she thought marriage and children were the holy grails
of life. She didn't seem to get that when you were doing
the work you'd been born to do, a family sometimes
seemed more like dessert than the main course.

Not that he didn't enjoy the company of a woman
now and then. And Amber had her charms. He found
her intelligent, attractive and pleasant company. Fortunately she was easygoing, as well, since so far he'd had
to cancel three of their seven dates.

He'd told her he would call her when he got home
but it had been five hours since the crackers and cheese
Maddie Turner had fed him and he was getting light-
headed.

Farley took out a full carton of eggs and a loaf of
bread. He felt as if he could eat all of this and more.
It had been a while since he'd used his fancy kitchen
to its full potential. Maybe on the weekend he'd invite
Amber over for dinner.

But when Farley tried to imagine Amber standing by
the stove or sitting across from him at the table, all he
could see was golden-haired Cassidy. Sweet as honey
one minute. As fired up as a bumblebee the next.

Easygoing did not describe Cassidy. But she was so
deliciously *alive*. She'd been around seventeen when

he'd stopped seeing her as a spunky little girl and saw her as a desirable woman. He could still remember the exact moment. He'd been watching TV with her brothers when she'd come down the hall dressed in a jean skirt and T-shirt. Her long blond hair had been freshly washed, and she'd been wearing makeup—for the first time that he'd ever noticed.

Wow, he'd thought. He hadn't stared, but it had taken all of his self-control not to. She was too young. The sister of his best friends. He knew his feelings weren't appropriate and he'd done his best to deny them.

But when he saw her at the bar on her twenty-first birthday, he hadn't been able to resist asking her out. The date started perfectly. Olive had smiled at him warmly when he arrived to pick up Cassidy, letting him know that she approved of him dating her only daughter.

And Cassidy had looked beautiful—quieter than usual—but absolutely lovely. They'd danced the first set as if they were the only two people in the room— gazes fused, bodies coming together like two pieces of an interlocking puzzle.

And then she'd asked for a drink and by the time he returned with the requested glass of punch, she was dancing with someone else.

This had all happened a long time ago. Four years. He'd thought he'd put it all behind him.

But then he'd seen her today and he'd felt the old punch of attraction.

What had been up with that? It didn't make sense. Once Cassidy Lambert had seemed like his dream girl.

But the reality was different. She'd grown up into a spoiled brat who treated men like dirt and wanted to live the high life in the city. Not that he had anything against city folk. But he sure had no use for a woman like that in his life.

Chapter Five

Cassidy got up around three in the morning to check on Lucy, then again at dawn. Both times the horse seemed to be holding her own, no better, no worse. By six o'clock, Cassidy was hungry. Usually they had oatmeal or boiled eggs and toast for breakfast, but wanting to surprise her mother—and make a special effort to please her—Cassidy decided to cook crepes using a recipe Josh had taught her.

She passed Corb and Jackson on her way from the home barn to the house. They were heading out to the cow and equestrian barns, respectively.

"Want to join Mom and me for breakfast later? I'm planning something special."

"*You're* cooking? No, thanks."

She smacked her brother's shoulder. "I'm better than I used to be." She had a reputation for burning anything she tried to make, thanks to her impatient habit of cooking everything on high heat so it would be ready faster.

"I'm sure you are. I was just kidding. But I want to head back home and make Laurel something to eat when I'm finished here. She had a rough night with the baby."

"What about you, Jackson?"

"I'm kind of tied up today," her foster brother mumbled. "Thanks, anyway."

"Okay, fine, boys. Your loss. I'm making crepes." She thought that might tempt them, but both men just kept walking. Corb, she could understand—she was actually proud that he'd turned into such a caring husband and father—but Jackson lived alone. You'd think he might enjoy a little company and a meal he didn't have to cook for himself.

In the old days, when their father was alive, Jackson had seemed like another brother to her. But lately—and most particularly since the accident—he'd been distant. Cassidy didn't think it was only to her and she made a mental note to talk to Corb about this.

In the kitchen Cassidy put on a pot of coffee, then whipped up the batter, prepared the fruit and started a small nonstick frying pan on medium-low heat.

When her mother came in from her morning "rounds" as she liked to call them, Cassidy had a stack of crepes ready. She waved a hand at the table. "Sit down, Mom. I'm waiting on you for a change."

"What's this?" Olive looked from the table, to the stove, to her daughter.

"I made you breakfast." Cassidy handed her mother a cup of coffee with the cream and sugar already added. Then she plated two crepes with some fruit salad and set it down along with the pitcher of syrup.

"Well. Isn't this something."

Cassidy waited for her mother to take a taste.

Olive took a tentative bite. "Sweet, isn't it?"

"Is it too sweet?"

"I wouldn't say that. Stop standing there, watching me. Aren't you going to eat, too?"

Cassidy joined her mother, and dug into the meal

with a keen appetite. Must be all the fresh air and the hard work from yesterday. When she was finished, she went to the stove to help herself to seconds.

"Can I give you some more, Mom?"

"I don't think so, sweetheart. This was lovely, but I find eggs and toast and oatmeal stick to the ribs when you have a long day ahead of you."

"Oh."

"Since the frying pan is already out, I think I'll cook a few eggs. Want me to put some on for you?"

"No, thanks." She put the syrup back in the fridge and her plate in the dishwasher. It was silly for her to have hurt feelings because her mother preferred a more robust morning meal.

She wondered when Corb and Laurel were going to tell their mother about Winnie's baby. "Any plans to see Corb today?"

"No. I'm leaving in about thirty minutes to negotiate a sale of some of our yearlings with a rancher out Lewistown way. If the meeting goes too long, I may end up taking a room in town and coming home in the morning."

"What about the quarantine?"

"Yes." Her mother sighed with annoyance. "We'll have to delay delivery until that's cleared up, I guess."

"Speaking of clearing it up, I'm going out now to check on the rest of the horses."

An egg splattered as her mother added it to the hot frying pan. "Good. If any of them seem even a little off, make sure you call Farley right away."

"Mom thinks Farley walks on water," Cassidy confided to Sky as they headed out of the house toward the pasture. "So do my brothers."

Sky cocked her head as if to say, *Go on.* Cassidy did.

"Well, he is a pretty good vet. I'll give him that. But most eligible bachelor in Bitterroot County? That has to be stretching things."

Cassidy's mood lightened when she spotted the ranch's working horses munching on the hay Jackson had rolled out for them earlier. She slipped between the rungs of the wooden fence.

"You stay here, Sky," she told the border collie, and Sky promptly lowered onto her haunches.

Cassidy had grown up with most of these horses and considered them just as much family as she did Sky… and her brothers. She made the rounds, saying hello to each and every one of them, at the same time checking for signs of the dreaded strangles.

Finally she came to her own coffee-colored mustang, Finnegan. She'd owned him since she was eight, and he was now twenty-one years old.

"Hey, old man. How come you're not chowing down with the others?" She offered him a hunk of a carrot she'd snatched from the fridge earlier. Finnegan just gave it a sniff.

She patted his neck and some of his light brown hair went flying. "You could use some pretty serious grooming, huh?" In fact, all of the horses were looking scruffy.

"Hey, Cass!"

She swiveled, following the sound of Corb's voice. He'd just left the cattle barn and was walking in her direction.

"If you have time today, they could all use a little action with the shedding shears."

"I noticed."

"It's been hard without Brock." Corb shrugged. "We

can't seem to get enough done in a day, despite the extra workers B.J. hired."

Their eldest brother had returned to the rodeo circuit a week after Brock's funeral. Cassidy suspected he'd hired the extra workers to assuage his guilt for leaving them all so quickly.

Not that she'd been any better. She'd gone right back to school, hoping she could run from the heartbreak of losing her brother.

Focusing on her studies had helped some, but she'd spent a lot of tearful nights. "I guess it would take more than one hired wrangler to replace our brother out here," Cassidy said sadly, eyeing the neglected herd.

"Jackson used to take care of these guys as well as handling all the admin work and accounting. But I asked him to step in and manage the breeding program, so he's pretty much run ragged these days."

"Is that why he's being so standoffish?"

"Overwork?" Corb gave the idea less than two seconds of thought. "No. I think he still feels guilty about the accident."

"But it wasn't his fault. There was nothing he could have done." Savannah Moody had made that clear after the investigation was completed and no charges had been laid.

"He still blames himself, and I guess I understand how he feels. I'd probably feel the same in his shoes."

"Have you tried talking to him?"

"Of course I have. But it doesn't help that Mom is treating him even more coldly than she used to."

For some reason their mother hadn't been keen when her husband came up with the idea of taking on a foster son. But while Bob Lambert usually gave in to whatever Olive wanted, on this point he'd been surprisingly firm, and Jackson had come to Coffee Creek Ranch where her father had treated him the same as one of his own.

"If only Dad was still with us. He'd know what to say to make Jackson feel better."

"Maybe he could." Corb sighed. "But we might as well wish the accident had never happened. Dad and Brock are both gone and we have to deal with it."

He glanced at Cassidy then, and she wondered if he thought her plans to work in Billings were selfish, when she was so obviously needed here.

"Do we have the money to hire more help?"

Corb nodded. "When Jackson moved to the breeding program, the plan was to find a new accountant so he wouldn't have to bother with the desk work anymore. But so far Mom hasn't given the go-ahead on that."

Cassidy could guess why. Her mother expected *her* to fill that role.

"I'll do what I can to help while I'm here, Corb. But I can't stay. I worked hard for my degree and I want a chance to use it."

Besides, after living apart from her mother the past five years, she could never go back to living in the same house as her.

The crepes episode was a perfect example of how a simple little thing could get her all upset. Life was too short to keep doing that to herself.

"I just couldn't come back here to live. I'm sorry."

"Hey." Corb patted her shoulder. "I didn't mean to make you feel guilty. I get it."

"By the way, you'll have to wait to tell Mom about Winnie's baby. She's off to Lewistown today and may not be home until tomorrow."

"Thanks for letting me know that." He stepped back

from her and gave the horses a good look-over. "So how do they seem to you? Any signs of strangles?"

"Nothing obvious. But I noticed Finnegan seems to be off his food. He didn't even want the carrot I just offered him." She unclenched her fist, where the untouched chunk of carrot still sat.

"Damn." Corb checked the mustang more closely, then shook his head. "Doesn't look sick to me, but just to be sure, we better put him up in a separate area of the barn. Keep him away from both Lucy and the other horses."

Cassidy nodded. She'd already decided the same thing, though she was almost positive that Finnegan didn't have strangles. He couldn't.

Still, she brought him into the barn, settling him into the stall farthest from Lucy's. An hour later Corb and two hired hands tacked up four horses and went out to sort calves for branding. Cassidy busied herself cleaning Lucy's stall and hauling the soiled hay away and burning it as per Farley's orders.

Two hours later, she had to admit that Finnegan was looking worse. She'd offered him some oats and given him a thorough grooming, but he still wasn't eating and seemed decidedly lackluster.

Much as she didn't want to, she could see no alternative.

She had to call Farley.

CASSIDY MADE THE call from the barn, using the phone in the office where she and Farley had talked just one day earlier. She'd hoped to clear the air with him then, but the truth was she felt even more awkward now than she had before.

So she was relieved when his phone was answered by someone else.

"Farley & Sons," said a woman with a brisk, no-nonsense voice. "Liz speaking."

Even though Farley now worked on his own, he hadn't changed the name of the business to reflect this. "Hi. This is Cassidy Lambert from Coffee Creek Ranch. Farley was out here yesterday looking at one of our horses."

"*Cassidy* Lambert?"

"Yes."

"I see."

Was it her imagination or did the woman's voice shift from businesslike to frosty?

"Well, if you're wondering about the test results for your palomino, it's going to take several days before we know for sure."

"I was actually calling because we have a second horse off his feed and I was wondering if Farley could come take a look at him."

"Dan has a full schedule today. And plans for dinner with his girlfriend tonight."

Dan Farley had a girlfriend? She knew she shouldn't be surprised, or even interested, but she was both. Fighting the urge to ask questions that weren't appropriate, Cassidy refocused on the issues that *did* matter.

"This second horse is older, and I'm afraid if he has strangles it could hit him hard. I'd really appreciate it if Farley could come as soon as possible."

"Well, he could maybe squeeze in a visit tomorrow. He was planning to swing by Silver Creek then, anyway."

Tomorrow. Cassidy hated to wait that long. But it

didn't seem she had any choice. "Do they have strangles at Silver Creek, too?"

"Not at all. Far as we know, you're the only ones in the area."

Which meant the mystery of how Lucy had contracted the bacterial infection was still unsolved. Maybe it *had* been that secondhand tack. Cassidy ended the unsatisfactory call and went back to check on the horses.

While she was applying a fresh compress to Lucy's neck, Corb and the hired men came back with their horses. They looked dirty and tired and she offered to brush down their horses and clean the tack for them.

The men gave her grateful smiles, passing off their horses before taking off for their well-deserved dinners.

Careful to protect the horses from infection, Cassidy brushed them off outside before letting them loose in the pasture. Then she turned to the tedious job of disinfecting the tack room. The job took several hours and she was tired, sweaty and hungry by the time she was finished. Still, rather than head in for the shower and meal that she craved, she washed thoroughly and went back to Finnegan.

There wasn't much light left in the day at that point, but she didn't need it to see that Finnegan had deteriorated. He had discharge in his nostrils and he still hadn't touched either the oats, the carrot or the hay she'd left out for him.

Heck and darn.

Lucy was doing worse, too. Not only were the glands in her neck visibly more swollen, but she seemed to be struggling with each breath.

Mentally Cassidy went over the instructions Farley had left with her and wondered if she'd missed something. She wished she had someone to ask, but it was past eight o'clock now and there was no one around. She could always call Corb at the cabin. But he had no more experience with strangles than she did, and he already had precious little time to spend with his wife and baby daughter.

Liz had said Farley might make it tomorrow morning.

So she'd just hang on until then.

"Looks like it's going to be a long night," she said, speaking out loud as she set up the cot they used when keeping watch over pregnant mares. She made a pot of coffee in the office and found a box of granola bars stashed in a bottom filing cabinet. She ate one for herself and broke up a second for Sky.

They had an old radio in the barn tuned to a local country station and she put that on.

It helped to have a little music and the radio announcer for company, though she could have done without the ads, which were jarring at the best of times.

She wondered what Josh was doing and took her phone out of her back pocket. Two missed calls and three text messages.

Going out for lunch with Kate and Liam—two of their college friends. Then, an hour later, Wish you were here, too. And the final message, sent just fifteen minutes ago. You're quiet. What's up?

She thought about answering, but her heart wasn't in it. Josh had grown up in Great Falls and had never even owned a pet. He'd try to be sympathetic, but he wouldn't really understand why she was so upset. Besides, she didn't feel like talking. She hated to see any animal suffer and when they were animals she knew and loved it was even harder.

She sat on an overturned wooden bucket at the back

door of the barn, with one arm looped around Sky's neck. The sun was setting and the rolling hills to the west had never looked lovelier against the swirls of vivid orange and red.

"This must be the most beautiful place in the world, don't you think?"

For answer, her dog rested her muzzle on Cassidy's knee.

"They'll be okay, right? I mean, strangles isn't fatal." *At least not usually.* Gosh, she was tired. She'd only managed a few hours of sleep last night and today she'd been a lot more active than usual.

Thankfully the rest of the horses seemed fine. The four horses she'd groomed earlier were enjoying their evening feed with the rest of the small herd.

Once the sun was down, Cassidy decided she might as well try to catch a little sleep. Leaving on the lights in the office and the tack room, so she didn't feel quite so all alone, she sank onto the narrow mattress and closed her eyes.

A few minutes later she became aware of a high-pitched noise rising above the music on the radio. Sky growled and went to the closed barn door, whining to be let out.

Coyotes.

"Come back here, Sky. Ignore them."

It was a mark of Sky's obedience that she listened and returned to lie at the foot of Cassidy's cot.

But by the dog's uneasy stirrings, Cassidy could tell she wasn't going back to sleep. They'd always had coyotes here on the ranch. Just like moose, elk and white-tailed deer, they were part of the natural order.

But tonight their nighttime cries sounded closer than normal.

Eventually they quieted, though. Probably they'd moved on, farther down the valley.

Cassidy relaxed and finally drifted to sleep.

FARLEY WAS SURPRISED to find the Lamberts' house completely dark when he pulled up in his SUV at ten o'clock that evening. He felt like a fool for taking Amber home early after their dinner and for driving out all this way.

He started to pull a U-turn, then he noticed a couple of lights on at the home barn where Lucy was quarantined.

So he parked and grabbed his black kit from the passenger seat. A series of motion-activated lights illuminated the path for him as he made his way to the barn.

His boots crunched on the graveled path, mixing in with the chorus from the frogs in the nearby lake. As he drew closer to the barn a new sound rose softly in the night air.

He recognized the melancholic refrain of a popular country tune. The radio was on. He'd been listening to the same station on his drive over here.

Sky was waiting at the barn door for him. Where you found Sky, you were bound to find Cassidy, but at first he saw no sign of her.

Two horses nickered at him. One was Lucy. The other—at the opposite end of the barn—had to be the second horse Liz had reported Cassidy suspected was sick, too. A closer look told him it was Finnegan—the mustang Cassidy had ridden when she was growing up. This wasn't good news. Finnegan had to be getting on in years by now. The older horse would have a tougher time with strangles.

Once his eyes had adjusted to the low light in the stables, he finally spotted Cassidy. She was sleeping on a cot next to Finnegan's stall, curled up with a blanket that he'd seen in the office the other day.

A feeling that was both powerful and tender welled up in him. Why? It didn't seem to matter that she'd treated him like dirt. That she'd spurned his way of life. He wished like hell that he could transfer those feelings to Amber, a woman for whom such a longing would make a hell of a lot more sense.

The song ended, and the radio announcer started in on a weather update.

Cassidy's eyes slowly opened. She stared right at him. Blankly, at first. Then her eyes rounded and she whispered, "Farley? I can't believe you're here."

"Liz said it was an emergency." He turned away, fighting an impulse to hold out his hand and help her up.

She didn't need one anyway. Quickly she stood up, planting her feet—she hadn't taken off her boots—on the concrete floor. "What time is it?"

"About quarter after ten," he guessed.

"Really? Thanks for coming out so late."

"Don't worry about it," he said, brushing aside the thanks. "Just wait till your mother gets my next vet bill. You'll probably hear the shriek all the way to Billings."

"Well, it was still awfully nice of you." She was up now, moving to Finnegan, stroking the horse and crooning. "Hey, baby, don't worry. The vet's here now and he's going to help you." She turned to Farley.

His heart clenched at the sight of her face, and all that he could read in it. It seemed so genuine, her concern for her horse. But in a few more weeks she'd be in Billings—how much would she care then?

He put a hand on the mustang's flank and began his inspection. "How was he acting today?"

"Kind of listless. Wouldn't eat, not even his oats or

a carrot." She exhaled despairingly. "Everything you said to watch out for."

"Well, he is running a fever," he confirmed ten minutes later. "And there is a little clear discharge. I'll take a swab for testing, but I think in this case it would be smart to start on antibiotics right away. Maybe we've caught it early enough that it will help."

He moved to Lucy next. "How's our other patient doing?"

"She hasn't eaten much today, either. And starting late this afternoon, she seems to be struggling to breathe. I've been changing her hot compresses every twenty minutes—except when I fell asleep," she added guiltily.

"Lucy's having trouble breathing because those swollen lymph nodes are pressing right up against her airway. We need to relieve the pressure and soon."

"Poor Lucy. Should I get some more hot compresses?"

"No. I was hoping the abscesses would burst on their own, but since they haven't, we'll have to lance them."

"Will it hurt her?"

"Not if we do it right. Are you willing to help?"

She looked insulted. "Of course I am."

"It won't be pretty."

She put up her chin. "You don't think I can handle a little pus?"

"Not a little. A lot. And I don't know what you can handle, Cass. I just thought it was fair to warn you."

Chapter Six

Why did being around Farley always have to be so complicated? She'd been so relieved, at first, that he was here, and she was no longer alone with her worry and fear. True, she could have called Corb or Jackson, but handling the strangles outbreak was her responsibility and her brothers had already put in long days.

Besides, what could they have done that she wasn't already doing?

Farley was different. He was a vet, obviously. But he also had a calm, take-charge attitude. Just his presence was enough to make her feel better.

For a while. But it didn't take long for other emotions to tangle up her heart. She felt defenseless, confused... and even angry.

He had this disapproving way of looking at her that made her feel so small.

Yes, she'd behaved abominably at the Harvest Dance four years ago. But it had been four years. And she'd finally apologized.

So what was he holding against her now?

She felt sure it was something.

"I'll need some clean rags," Farley said as he pulled equipment from his open case. She saw a bottle of antiseptic, cotton swabs, a big, ugly-looking knife... Suddenly she felt woozy. She went for the rags, glad to have an excuse to look the other way for a while.

She'd put on a brave front, but the truth was she hated icky things like pus and vomit…and especially blood. But she would get past all of that tonight. She had to do it for a horse whose heart was as wide and open as the Montana skyline.

Cassidy's determination to be brave was sorely tested in the next twenty minutes. It was awful watching Farley cut through the abscess.

Lucy was a trouper throughout, a model patient, Farley said. And, fortunately, once the pus was gone, her breathing immediately returned to normal.

When it was done, he showed her how to prepare a tamed iodine solution.

"You'll need to flush the wound once a day to keep it clear of infection."

They were arm-to-arm as he said this. She could feel his warmth, the solid bulk of his broad shoulders against her slight ones.

"Like this." He demonstrated, then handed the solution and gauze to her.

She followed his example, feeling pleasure when he nodded his approval.

"Good job," he said. "Most people wouldn't have been able to stomach a procedure like this one."

"It was tough," she admitted. "But I was so worried about Lucy, I kind of put it out of my mind."

"I guess you haven't changed all that much, after all. Still can't stand to see an animal suffer."

Cassidy's breath caught in her throat. He was so close she could smell his cologne over the pungent odor of the iodine. But wait a minute. The scent was too sweet and floral to be something a man would wear.

And then she remembered what Liz had told her.

"So how was your date?"

Farley dropped his syringe, then recovered it from the straw bedding and tossed it in the bag containing all the pus-soaked rags. "What makes you think I was on a date?"

She followed her nose, which led her to the collar of his shirt. "It's either that, or you've started to wear Joy. Not the first choice for most men who wear cologne."

"Stop *sniffing* me."

She backed off, amused. "Why not? It's nice. I bought a bottle for Laurel this Christmas."

"I do *not* smell like perfume."

He was embarrassed, she noted with glee. "My mistake. It must be Lucy, that silly horse. I keep telling her the stallions prefer her natural pheromones."

Farley looked pained. And then he laughed. "If you must know, I was out for dinner with Amber Ellis. I had no idea she wore Joy perfume. But at least now I know what to get her for her birthday."

Amber Ellis. Corb had dated her a few years back. Cassidy remembered liking her a lot. So why did she feel this sudden flash of irritation toward her?

Farley packed up his bag, instructed her on the various medicines and treatments for the horses, then rolled up his sleeves and washed at the sink.

"Should I stay out here and keep an eye on them?" she asked, when what she really wondered was whether Farley would be heading home now...or to Amber's.

"We've done all we can for tonight. Go inside and get a decent night's sleep. They'll be okay until morning. In fact, I'm expecting Lucy will be a whole lot better by then."

Cassidy didn't ask about Finnegan. She was too afraid of getting the wrong answer.

THE NEXT MORNING Cassidy was up early to check the horses. As Farley had predicted, Lucy was much improved. Cassidy fed her warm mush, administered the antibiotics and mucked out the stalls. After, she burned the soiled bedding as before and disinfected the feed and water buckets.

There wasn't much she could do for Finnegan, though, who still had little appetite and the tell-tale strangles nasal discharge. While his glands hadn't swollen as much as Lucy's had, Cassidy prepared hot compresses for him anyway.

She was on her way back to the ranch house when she spotted Corb on the other side of the yard.

"Want to come out for a ride?" he asked. "I need to fix a section of fencing on the northern boundary."

The sun was shining in a cloud-free sky. There was nothing Cassidy would rather do. But she shook her head. "I better stay close to home and keep an eye on Finnegan."

"How's Lucy?"

"A lot better. Last night she was having trouble breathing but Farley came by and lanced the abscesses. She's almost her old self today."

"Farley came by, huh? Must have been pretty late. Now that's good service, I say."

Cassidy noticed the teasing gleam in her brother's eyes, but she knew how to keep him under control. "Yes. Unfortunately he had to cut his date with Amber Ellis a few hours short. You remember Amber, don't you, Corb?"

He flushed, just as she'd hoped he would. "You pest.

Better get to the kitchen. If you're not coming out riding today, Mom has some errands she wants you to run. She got back about an hour ago and is in the kitchen making a list."

"Before you saddle up any of the horses, make sure they seem healthy," she reminded him before she left. "Let me know if any of them aren't eating or seem listless."

"You got your phone on you?" he asked.

She nodded.

"Okay. I'll call you if there are any problems."

As she headed to the house, Cassidy wondered what mood her mother would be in. Olive had stopped by the barn earlier, making her morning rounds later than usual, as she'd spent the night in Lewistown. They hadn't talked much, though, since Olive hadn't wanted to risk spreading the strangles by stepping inside the barn.

Having their riding horses in quarantine was bad enough. It would be a disaster, though, if the quarter horses were infected.

She found her mother in the kitchen, making a fry-up in the huge cast-iron pan that had been in the family pretty much forever. Cassidy cringed as she thought of her crepe-making fiasco of the previous day. She should have known better than to try something new with her mother.

Mother only liked new ideas when she thought of them.

"Help yourself to coffee," Olive said. "This'll be ready in a minute. How's my Lucy doing?"

Cassidy caught her mother up with the latest developments, then listened to her mom talk horse prices while they ate their scrambled eggs mixed with sausage, tomatoes and onions. When they were finished, Olive asked her to move her belongings into Corb's old room.

"The painters are coming today."

"That was fast."

"The curtains and duvet cover won't be ready for a few weeks," Olive said. "But the new armoire is being delivered on Friday."

"New armoire?"

"I paid for it in Lewistown yesterday. After my meeting," she added, looking at her daughter as if she thought she was a little slow for not keeping up.

In Cassidy's opinion, the last thing they needed to be worrying about at this busy time of year was redecorating her bedroom, but she knew better than to complain. "That sounds great, Mom."

"Nothing is too much trouble for my kids." Her mother got up and patted Cassidy's cheek, then pulled out a shopping bag. "And look at what I found for Stephanie."

Inside were the tiniest pair of cowboy boots that Cassidy had ever seen. "Gosh, these are cute."

Also in the bag was a tiny jumper with Cowgirl printed on the front, a velvety-soft stuffed horse and a picture book about farm animals.

With the Lambert family, indoctrination started early.

"That's so nice, Mom." She set the bag aside, feeling a pang for the other new baby in the family. Corb better tell their mother soon. The longer they delayed, the worse Olive was going to take it.

Just then, her phone signaled an incoming text message. It was from Corb and the message was simple.

Tell her.

Heck and darn. Was he serious? Not my place, she texted back.

Please?

Cassidy sighed. She really did hate her mother not knowing this. "Mom? I found out something major last night when I dropped in on Corb and Laurel."

Olive frowned. "This sounds like bad news."

"More like a big surprise. Sit down, please."

She waited until her mother was actually in a chair before she continued. "You know how Winnie has been staying at her parents' because of health issues?"

"I always said that woman didn't have the strength to be a rancher's wife."

"Actually, she's had a good reason for not returning to Coffee Creek sooner. She was two months pregnant when Brock died."

Olive gasped and Cassidy jumped up to get her mother a glass of water.

"Winnie had a little boy in January."

"Brock's son?"

Cassidy nodded.

"Oh, my word.... Why didn't she tell us?"

"Think about it, Mom. Can you guess why she might have been reluctant?"

A rare flush rose on Olive's cheeks.

"She was grieving. And according to Laurel she had a very difficult pregnancy. So we've got to be understanding. Besides, if we get Winnie angry, we may lose out on the chance to be a part of Brock's baby's life."

Olive nodded slowly. "You're right."

"Good. So don't go doing or saying anything you might regret later."

Again Olive nodded. "I'll have to think about this."

"In the meantime, do you need anything from town?

Corb said you had a list of errands and I'm planning on going to the library this morning."

The radio had been good company last night. But a book would be even better.

"I do." Her mom handed her a shopping list. "And would you mind taking this outfit to Laurel?" She handed Cassidy the little cowgirl duds. "I can't believe I have another grandchild. Seems like I have a lot of shopping to catch up on."

CASSIDY TOOK SKY along with her for the drive into Coffee Creek. She went to the Cinnamon Stick first, and she and Laurel shared a laugh at the ranch-themed gifts from Olive.

"I'm not sure about the boots—I don't think Stephanie will be wearing shoes for a long time. But everything else is wonderful. Olive sure does like to spoil her granddaughter. We've had a gift from her almost every week since Steph was born."

"Hopefully they didn't come with too many strings attached."

Laurel raised her eyebrows, but didn't say anything further. After the way Olive had tried to commandeer the wedding plans for Laurel's marriage to Corb, Cassidy thought it was big of her not to add her own complaints to the list.

"By the way, Corb asked me to tell Mom about Winnie's son. So I did it."

"Really?" Laurel's eyes grew huge. "How did she take it?"

"I didn't give her much of a chance to react. I just warned her that if we didn't treat Winnie very carefully we might end up not being part of Brock's son's life. I left her to mull that over for a while."

"Gosh. I have to call Winnie and let her know that Olive's been told. She'll be glad she didn't have to be the one."

"Does she have any plans to bring the baby back to Coffee Creek?"

"Eventually," Laurel said. "But I don't think she's ready yet. On top of all the other problems she's had, it seems her son is really colicky."

Laurel handed her a cup of coffee. "So how was your night? Corb tells me that Farley dropped by for a while? He also said that Farley is dating Amber Ellis."

"Really? He passed that along already?"

Laurel smiled smugly. "Text message about five minutes after you told him."

Cassidy laughed. "Well, at least the lines of communication are working in your marriage."

"That's all you have to say? What about Amber? Are you upset?"

"Why would I be?"

Laurel just raised her eyebrows.

Cassidy took her coffee in a to-go cup, plus a bag containing several cinnamon buns that Laurel pressed on her. She certainly wasn't going to admit, not even to Laurel, that she didn't like the idea of Farley dating Amber one little bit.

Cassidy headed to the library next. Every time she entered the historic old building she wished she'd been alive when the children of the area had all gone to school here. A one-room schoolhouse combining six grades' worth of pupils must have been a lot of fun.

The librarian, Tabitha Snow, was on her computer when Cassidy arrived. She broke out in a welcoming smile and left her desk to give Cassidy a hug. "You're back! How did it go?"

"Very well. Though I must admit I'm glad to put all that intense studying behind me. I'd like to read something fun for a change."

It was nice to see Tabitha again. She'd encouraged Cassidy's love of books and learning from an early age. But it was a little disconcerting as well to see new gray hairs and tiny lines around the attractive librarian's mouth. A reminder that things had changed in the years she'd been away from Coffee Creek.

"Oh, I know just the story. This one kept me up all hours last week." She pulled a book from a wheeled cart next to her desk. "And the ending is perfectly wonderful—you never see it coming but it feels so true when it happens."

Cassidy gave the back cover a quick read and agreed it sounded interesting. "Thanks, I'll take it." She dug her library card out of her pocket and handed it over, interested to see that even their small local library had gone electronic, with bar codes, scanners and everything.

"So how are things with you?"

"Oh, the same." Tabitha looked surprised that she would even ask. "I adopted a new cat this fall. That makes six now." She sighed. "I suppose I'm becoming something of a cliché. The old lady who lives alone with her cats and her books. Next thing you know I'll take up crocheting."

"Why not? Since Winnie went to live with her folks, she's taken up knitting. And what's wrong with cats and books, anyway? Both sound like wonderful things to surround yourself with."

"Ah, you always were the sweetest child. Not a child anymore, of course, but I'm glad you kept the sweet part." Tabitha handed her the book. "There you go. You have three weeks, but if you like the story as much as I did, I predict you'll be back within a few days."

As it happened, Cassidy left the library at the same time as the postmaster from the building next door was crossing the street for his usual lunch at the Cinnamon Stick.

"Hey, Burt."

"Cassidy." He nodded.

Three years ago Burt and Tabitha had been married. When they separated they set up rules so they could continue to live in the same small town without causing each other too much grief.

One of their agreements was that Tabitha would frequent the Cinnamon Stick in the morning, and Burt at noon. That way they wouldn't have to worry about running into one another.

Cassidy had assumed the arrangement was temporary, but it seemed they were still sticking to their schedule. "Any mail for Coffee Creek Ranch today, Burt?" she called out across the street.

"Nope. Your mother picked it up yesterday afternoon on her way to Lewistown." He nodded again, then disappeared inside the café.

Cassidy shrugged, then continued to her truck, which she'd parked outside of the café. She was surprised to see Maddie Turner standing at the open passenger-side window, petting Sky. She was so short, Cassidy didn't see her until she was only a few feet away. Sky had sure noticed Maddie's presence, though. She was wiggling, panting and smiling, the way she always did when greeting a friend.

Cassidy stopped, not sure what to do.

When she was growing up, she had witnessed both her mother and her father cross the street rather than exchange a greeting with Maddie. She herself had never spoken to the woman who was her aunt.

But to ignore her now seemed just plain silly.

"Hi. My dog sure seems to like you."

"I hope you don't mind. I couldn't resist stopping to say hello. And it seems like she remembers me." Maddie's voice sounded hoarse. She pulled out a tissue and coughed.

"Corb mentioned something about Sky coming from a litter of yours."

"That's right. Her mother was a direct descendant of the border collie your mother and I had when we were growing up."

Cassidy frowned. "So how exactly did I come to own her?"

Though her dog had been delivered to their door in a basket on her fourteenth birthday, she'd always assumed her father was behind the gift.

Maddie smiled shyly. "I had a feeling you would like one another. Was I right?"

Cassidy didn't know what to say. She was surprised that Maddie Turner even knew her birth date, let alone that she would have given her such a special gift. She wondered if her mother had guessed that the dog had been from her sister. Given the breed, she probably had. So maybe that was why she had been so annoyed.

"I don't know what to say. Thank you. Sky was my best friend when I was growing up." She thought for a moment. "And she still is."

"That's the way I feel about my dogs, as well. I have two border collies on Silver Creek—"

Maddie stopped abruptly, her gaze shifting to the door of the café, where Vince Butterfield, the ex-bronc rider turned baker, was just stepping out at the end of his shift.

"Hello, Maddie," Vince said, his voice deep and rusty. "It's good to see you. Next time you're in for coffee you should come back to the kitchen and say hello."

Cassidy was surprised. Vince hardly ever did anything more than nod at the people he met. She glanced back at her aunt and was surprised to see that pain had clouded over Maddie's lovely eyes.

"I don't think so, Vince." Without another word to either of them she turned and walked away.

WHEN CASSIDY RETURNED home, her mother's SUV was in its usual parking space in front of the garage. Cassidy pulled in beside it and went inside through the back patio doors.

Her mother was just hanging up the phone and seemed startled to see her. "Oh, hi, sweetheart. How was the trip to Coffee Creek?"

"Great. Laurel said thanks for the gift. And she sent you back this." She handed her mother the bag with the cinnamon buns. "Who was that on the phone?"

"Oh—it was nothing important." Olive glanced at the cinnamon buns, then set the bag on the counter. "I've already had my lunch. I'm off for another meeting this afternoon. The Heritage Site Committee again."

Which explained why her mother had changed from the jeans she'd been wearing earlier, to the Western-styled skirt she had on now. Plus, she'd touched up her makeup.

"You look pretty, Mom."

"Thank you, dear." Olive picked up her satchel, then hesitated. "Would you consider joining the committee? We have a treasurer but she doesn't seem to know much about investing money and we've got a fair amount of funds just sitting in a savings account. You would be a real asset."

Her mother looked so hopeful, Cassidy felt like a heel turning her down. "I'd be glad to give your treasurer some investing advice. But I can't join full-time since I'm moving to Billings. It would be too far to travel for regular meetings."

It seemed like every muscle in her mother's face tightened. "So that's still on then?"

"Why wouldn't it be? I haven't got the job yet. But I'm hopeful. And even if I don't get that position, I'm sure I'll find something else."

Her mother said nothing to that, just sighed and changed the subject. She gave Cassidy a list of chores to do for the afternoon, including checking on the quarantined horses, which Cassidy had been intending to do anyway.

Once Olive had driven off, Cassidy went to the phone and scrolled through the recently called list. She had a funny feeling about that look she'd surprised on her mother's face. Sure enough, Josh's number topped the list of recent callers. Scrolling back further, she noticed he'd phoned her yesterday, too.

She pulled out her cell phone and hit his speed dial number.

"Finally!" He sounded breathless above the background noise of city bustle. "Why haven't you answered any of my texts or phone calls?"

She didn't tell him that her mother hadn't passed along his messages, since she hadn't responded to his calls on her cell phone, either. "It's been crazy here. We've got strangles and all our riding horses have been quarantined."

"Strangles? What's that?"

"It's a very contagious bacterial disease that—well, it can be really serious. And I've been put in charge of making sure it doesn't spread and nursing the infected horses."

"Wow. Sounds like you could use some help…"

Cassidy ignored the hint. Josh had been keen to visit her family ranch for some time now, but she had her doubts on how well he would fit in. He'd never even been on a horse and knew nothing about the cattle business. She was afraid Corb and Jackson would have a field day with him. And her mother… Well, the fact that she hadn't told Cassidy about any of Josh's calls pretty much demonstrated the sort of welcome *she* would give Josh if he came.

"I'm doing okay. What's new with you?"

"I got the second interview! I've been dying to tell you. We set a date for next week. How about you? Have you heard anything?"

"Not yet." She wouldn't put it past her mother not to tell her if she had, but she hadn't seen any calls from the firm on the recently called list. Besides, she'd given her cell phone number and email as her primary contact information. The home number was just for backup.

"Not to worry," Josh assured her. "I'm sure you'll hear something soon. Oh—and you should check for your marks. Mine were posted last night."

He reeled off a list of marks that were all impressive.

"Good for you. Look, Josh, I've got to go. I'll call you later when I have time to talk, okay?"

She hurried to her computer and went online. In minutes she was relieved to see that her final marks were even better than Josh's.

So why had he gotten the call while she was still waiting?

Deciding it was too soon to worry, she changed and was heading out to the barn, when she was intercepted by Jay Owen, one of their hired workers.

"We've got another sick horse," the short, wiry wrangler told her. "Chickweed. I just put him into the stall next to Finnegan."

Chapter Seven

The one person Cassidy didn't expect to see in the barn examining the newest sick horse was Farley. She watched him, unseen for a while. Despite his height and his broad shoulders, Farley was light on his feet and sure with his movements. If you could call a vet graceful, then Farley was graceful.

A slight movement from Sky, as always in her shadow, betrayed her presence.

Farley glanced up from the vial he was putting in his case. "Looks like we have another one."

"Oh, no. But you sure got here fast. I didn't even have time to call you."

"I was already on the property doing some preg testing in the cattle barn."

Since a grove of pine trees separated the cattle barn from the house, that explained why she hadn't seen his truck.

"That was lucky for us. So how is Chickweed doing?" The sturdy quarter horse was her brother Corb's favorite. They'd had him about ten years.

"Hey there, Chickweed." She patted the horse as she walked around him, doing a quick visual exam. Chickweed was a smart, sure-footed horse with terrific cow sense.

But she could tell right away, by his posture and the position of his neck and his head, that he wasn't feeling well. "Is he running a fever?"

"Afraid so. And he's definitely suffering some pain—see how swollen he is under his jaw?" Farley placed her hand over the enlarged lymph nodes, and she nodded.

Not only did she feel the evidence of strangles in the horse, but she also felt the rough calluses of Farley's hand. And the strength. And the warmth.

She remembered what his hands had felt like on her waist and on her shoulder, when they'd danced together four years ago. She'd never forgotten and never would.

Did he ever think about the good part of that night? Or just her inexcusable behavior afterward?

She glanced at his face, and saw that he was looking at her, his dark gaze as always intense, but inscrutable.

"Should I prepare some hot compresses?" she asked.

He blinked. "Yes."

The moment between them—if indeed, it had been a moment—was over. Farley went to his vet truck to get some more antibiotics, while she warmed up compresses for all three of her patients.

Lucy was restless as Cassidy washed her dried-up abscesses and when Cassidy offered her the warm oat mush, she gobbled it up.

"She's definitely feeling better," Cassidy noticed.

Finnegan, unfortunately, seemed to be worse. He ate only a few mouthfuls of the mush and hardly reacted when she called out his name and tried to give him a little loving.

"This is odd," Cassidy said. "His neck isn't as swollen as Lucy's was or as Chickweed's is right now, yet of all of them, he seems the sickest."

"You have to remember he's older," Farley reminded her. "And it's possible…"

"What?"

Farley removed the latex gloves he'd been wearing and tossed them into the trash. "There can be various complications from strangles. We'll have to keep a close eye on Finnegan."

"What sort of complications? What should I watch for?"

But Farley was frustratingly vague. "Just let me know if anything changes, okay?" He was at the doorway now. "I should get back to those cows. You okay in here?"

She was. But she liked it better when he was here with her.

Which was odd considering how much he disliked her.

"I'm fine," she insisted.

He hesitated before leaving. "Heard anything about that job in Billings?"

"Not yet. But I got the results from my finals and they were good."

"Congratulations."

"Still no word from the accounting firm, though. Some of my fellow students have already been called. Maybe I won't be getting a second interview."

Farley's gaze dropped to her boots, then returned to her eyes. He gave her a small smile—a shadow of the ones she could remember from earlier days—and nodded. "I'll bet you will."

FARLEY PULLED ON a pair of OB coveralls and disinfected his boots before rejoining Corb in the cattle barn. It was breeding season and Corb needed to know which of his cows were pregnant and which were not. It was messy, physical work that required Farley's full concentration.

Corb's job was lining up the cows for examination, then sorting them into pens when they were done.

"No wonder we pay you the big bucks," Corb said, as Farley unblocked an unusually large amount of fecal matter from one of the cows.

Farley shrugged. He was used to this. And the hard work was good distraction from a woman who could mess up his mind without even trying. Seeing how much she cared about her horses was making it hard for him to keep up the distance he'd planned with her. He'd assumed that part of her had calcified—around about the time she discovered how much fun she could have playing one guy off another.

But now he knew it hadn't.

She was as soft-hearted as ever.

Which meant that it was just him she had a problem with.

Self-preservation required that he stop noticing all the sweet, womanly things about her. But he couldn't seem to stop himself. He loved the soft curve of her ear that was exposed when she pulled back her hair, the incredible green of her eyes, the way she drew in one brow when she was confused or disbelieving.

The phone on his belt clip vibrated, reminding him that he still hadn't answered last night's phone message from Amber. She was the woman he should be thinking about right now. So why wasn't he?

He knew he owed her, at the least, a phone call. But how was he supposed to pursue a relationship with one woman, when he was all the time thinking about another?

He felt the small, squishy sac of the cow's uterus and

something harder inside, about the size of a baseball. "She's pregnant."

"Great." Corb released the animal with the other bred cows and Farley moved on to the next one.

If only women were as easy to understand as cows. He knew one thing for sure. His life would be a lot less complicated once Cassidy took that job and made a permanent move to Billings.

It was a long week for Cassidy. Chickweed turned out to be lucky. His case of strangles was mild and within seven days both he and Lucy seemed as good as new. Finnegan was different. His spirits dragged. His appetite was sporadic. Though terribly worried about her mustang, Cassidy was growing weary of her assignment, which kept her cooped up in the barn when she really wanted to be outside enjoying the warm May weather.

During her long nightly vigils—she refused to sleep in the house until she knew all the horses were out of danger—she'd finished the book Tabitha had recommended and another besides.

While the stories were pleasant diversions, she still felt increasingly restless. Plus she was getting really sick of the smell of disinfectant.

She could have spent more time in the house, rather than the barn, but she was also avoiding her mother who, when she wasn't complaining about Winnie keeping Brock's son a secret, was stepping up her campaign to get Cassidy to join the Coffee Creek Heritage Site Committee.

"We could schedule our meetings to coincide with your visits home," she'd offered last night during dinner.

"I don't think so, Mom."

"But why? Don't you care about this community? You could make a real difference here."

Her mother had gone on, talking about the importance of remembering the past and keeping alive the cowboy tradition. It was as if she was purposefully ignoring the fact that Cassidy planned to work as an accountant and live in Billings.

Though even that plan was beginning to look doubtful.

She *still* hadn't been called for a second interview and the waiting was driving her mad. Her marks had been top of the class, even better than Josh's. She'd thought she'd done well at the first interview.

So why wasn't she getting the second interview invitation that Josh and several other classmates had received?

Cassidy stopped to kick a wooden fence post. Just because she felt like it.

"Did it help?"

Heck and darn, Farley had seen her. He must be here doing more preg testing today. She hadn't seen his vet truck, but he'd probably parked it by the cattle barn again.

"Not really," she admitted.

"What's the problem?"

Even in an OB uniform covered with cow manure, Farley still looked ridiculously handsome. Something about those regal Native American cheekbones and his jet-black hair, which always fell perfectly in place and didn't even seem to show the indent from his hat when he removed it from his head.

Speaking of hair, hers was a mess. Something her mother had pointed out yesterday and again today.

"Just because you're living on a ranch doesn't mean you should get sloppy with your appearance, Cassidy."

"Spring fever," she said, after taking a moment to consider Farley's question. "I think Lucy and Chickweed have it, too. They're itching to get some exercise but I'm afraid to let them out with the other horses."

"Can't do that until we know they're not contagious," he agreed. "But they looked pretty spirited to me the last time I examined them. We could take them out for a ride. Clear their cobwebs—and our own, besides."

She glanced at him, intrigued by what she thought he'd just suggested. "*We* could take them? You have time for a trail ride?"

Even more surprising was the idea that he would want to go for a ride with *her* along for company.

He smiled. "I think I deserve a reward after all the cows I've felt up the past few weeks."

Cassidy didn't know who was happier to finally be free—her or Lucy. Farley on Chickweed was right behind them as they left the barn behind, then the yard, and then the pasture. It felt great to be out on the open range, knowing they could ride for hours and not run into another human being.

After ten minutes of pure exuberance, Cassidy brought Lucy down a couple of notches. "Easy, girl. I know you're happy to be out of that barn, but I don't want you to get sick again."

She turned to look at Farley, who was also transitioning Chickweed into a slower pace.

Cassidy couldn't help noticing…he'd cleaned up crazy good.

Gone were the gooey overalls and the latex gloves.

Now Farley was in faded jeans and a mossy-green shirt and a hat about as dark as his hair.

He looked sexy, handsome and just a little dangerous.

Just the way he'd looked to her four years ago at that dance. Back then the feelings had been more than she could handle. Now she couldn't help wondering what it would be like to kiss him.

Not that she saw it happening.

But what was the harm in a little daydreaming?

He urged Chickweed closer. "You and Lucy were made for one another."

"I feel that way, too. But she's my mother's horse."

"Yeah." He eyed the palomino thoughtfully. "But she's so agile. She'd make a lovely barrel racer."

"I *know*. I think the very same thing."

"Didn't you compete in high school?"

"Yes, with Finnegan. Much as I love my boy, though, I think Lucy has it all over him in the raw talent category. Not that it matters. I really can't imagine Mom taking up barrel racing any time soon."

"Your mother is in great shape for her age. But barrel racing? I don't think so."

"What about you? Do you still steer wrestle?"

"Every now and then," he admitted. "To let off a little steam."

"I remember watching you and my brothers practice. It used to scare me. I was so sure one of you was going to get hurt."

"Trust me, the hits were a lot easier to take when we were younger. I don't know how B.J. can keep up the pace he does. He called me the other day. Tried to talk me into registering in Central Point at the end of the month."

"The Wild Rogue Rodeo? Are you going to do it?"

"I might. What about you?"

For a moment she was tempted. Then she shrugged. "It's difficult for me to think about the future right now. Each day that passes without a call for that second interview just makes me realize how much I was counting on landing that job."

"You didn't look too worried a minute ago."

She hesitated. Then laughed. "That's true. Thanks for suggesting we do this. Isn't it a beautiful day? I mean, look at that view of Square Butte." She waved her hand at the mountain rising from the hills to their left. "Doesn't it just take your breath away?"

"I know what you mean." His voice sounded thoughtful, and she turned to look at him, trying to figure out his mood. He was looking at her, though, not the mountain.

Was he changing his mind about her?

"Forgiven me yet?" she dared to ask.

"Thinking about it."

"Yeah? What else are you thinking about? You looked so serious there for a minute."

"I was just wondering what made you choose accounting as your field of study?"

She had a feeling he'd pulled that question out of his hat, but she answered anyway. "Math was my best subject. The guidance counselor at school suggested I study business and the program at the U of M looked interesting."

"And did you enjoy it?"

She shrugged. The classes on accounting, statistics, management and finance had come easily to her. "I was good at it."

"Math and science were my best subjects, too. Did you ever consider something else like, say, vet school?"

"Mom mentioned the idea," she admitted. "But as you've already seen, I'm too squeamish."

"Yet, you have a way with animals. Your dog. Your horses."

"Yes. But I love them so much I can't stand to see them suffer." A vet had to have the ability to be rational and objective. She could never stand back dispassionately when an animal was hurting. "I even have a hard time helping with branding. I know it's necessary, that the calves don't hurt for long, but it always breaks my heart, all the same."

"And here I thought you were so tough."

"Did you really?"

"I remember you jumping off the bluffs on the far side of Cold Coffee Lake. That's a thirty-foot drop."

"Brock dared me."

"You were only ten years old at the time." He shook his head as if he still couldn't believe it.

"And scared to death," she confessed. "But it was fun after the first time." When it came to her *own* safety, she could be daring enough. It was the suffering of others— particularly helpless animals—that got to her the most.

They talked some more.

Farley told her about going to university, then vet school. He talked about his parents and how they'd decided to move to Arizona when he turned thirty.

"One thing I'll always be grateful for. My dad sat me down for a talk when I finished high school. He told me that while my grandfather and father had both been vets, I shouldn't feel pressured to follow in their footsteps. He told me I could do whatever I wanted with my life, and even though I had no doubt about choosing the veterinary field, I was always grateful to him for making sure I knew I had a choice."

"Wow," Cassidy said. "I couldn't imagine my mother having a talk like that with any of us kids."

"She wants you all to work at Coffee Creek."

"You noticed that, too, huh?"

He laughed, and after a second, so did she.

At one point Cassidy noticed a movement in some brush about twenty yards in the distance. The long grass swished and she caught a glimpse of gray. "Was that a coyote?"

"Yup. The females are nursing the young in their dens this time of year. Which means the males have been booted out and are feeling a little nastier than usual. There seem to be more around than usual. I was at Straws Monahan's the other day and he said they lost a couple barn cats last week. They suspected a coyote was involved."

"Oh, those poor kitties. I heard the coyotes howling last night. I was safe in the barn, yet even so it was kind of spooky."

"They won't bother us on the horses," Farley assured her.

It was Farley who first noticed the time. "We'd better head back. I should check in with my office. Liz will be having a fit."

"She likes to keep a tight rein on you," Cassidy said, remembering how protective the other woman had been on the phone, how quick to tell her that Farley was dating Amber Ellis.

"Too tight at times. But she's so darn good at what she does I put up with it." He glanced around the landscape. "It would be good to give the horses a drink. Is that a creek bed over there?"

Cassidy shielded her eyes and looked where he pointed, to a grassy bank and a large grove of shrubbery with some stunted pine trees, as well. They'd gained quite a lot of elevation and trees never grew as tall at this altitude.

"You're right. I think we've actually run up to the boundary of the Turner ranch. That's Silver Creek over there."

"Perfect." Farley signaled Chickweed to move toward the creek and Cassidy followed on Lucy. They dismounted by a clearing in the trees and let the horses free to drink their fill.

Cassidy scanned her surroundings, realizing that they'd ended up at the site of an old cattle shelter that had been used by the Turner family in the years when their operation had been as large as the Lamberts'.

Sure enough, on the other side of the creek, partially hidden by the bushy ponderosa pine, were the charred remains of an old barn.

Farley noticed it at the same time as she did. He whistled.

"This is the place where that vagrant died, isn't it?"

Cassidy nodded. B.J. and one of his buddies, Hunter Moody, had been out partying here with some friends when a storm blew in. Lightning had set the place on fire, and while all of B.J.'s friends had escaped without harm, unknown to them a young vagrant—passed out in the loft above their heads—had perished. The body had never been identified and everyone assumed the man was a vagrant from another state.

"I was only nine at the time, but I'll never forget Sheriff Smith coming to our door and taking B.J. and my dad in for questioning. I thought they'd been arrested and were going to jail and I'd never see them again."

"I was worried, too. Not that I believed B.J. had done

anything wrong, but my parents weren't keen on letting me hang out with your brothers for a while. A lot of people in the community believed B.J. and Hunter set that fire on purpose."

"Small towns and rumors." Cassidy shrugged them off. She knew her brother would never do anything like that. Still, she had a morbid impulse to check out the old barn. She decided to toss a challenge to Farley. "Want to take a look?"

He hesitated. "We'd have to cross the creek."

At the narrowest point, the creek was still a good eight feet across. And about two feet deep.

"We could do it on horseback," she replied.

"That we could."

They swung back up into their saddles, and Lucy and Chickweed gamely waded to the other side. As Cassidy dismounted, she realized this was the first time she'd ever set foot on Silver Creek Ranch property. Thinking back to her brief encounter with Maddie Turner earlier that day, she didn't think her aunt would mind.

"I'm amazed this place is still standing." Farley circled the charred structure, which was leaning decidedly to the east.

"Rain saved it from burning completely to the ground," Cassidy remembered.

"That's right. They said the vagrant died of smoke inhalation."

"I wonder if we'll ever know who he was."

"He must not have had any family, or someone would have tracked him down by now. I wouldn't suggest you go in there, Cass. It doesn't look safe."

"I agree." Cassidy took a last glance at the decrepit old barn, then whistled for Lucy.

Instead she found Farley. He'd moved closer to her

and was looking at her in a way that reminded her of that night four years ago.

She hitched her thumbs in the belt loops of her jeans, trying to pretend her heart hadn't suddenly started to pound.

He moved a little closer, this time near enough to reach out and touch the side of her face.

How could a finger so hard with calluses feel so tender?

"At the Harvest Dance…was that some game you were playing?"

"Why are you bringing that up again? I said I was sorry."

"That's fine. I'm still wondering why you did it. That guy. Did you ever see him again?"

"No. It wasn't about him. I just felt…over my head. That's all."

Understanding shone in his eyes then. "You were scared."

She nodded.

"There are nine years between us. It's a big gap."

"Back then it was." She could hardly believe she'd said that. As if to imply it *wasn't* a big gap now. That she and Farley…

"Well, it was probably just as well. If you hadn't pulled that stunt, I would have ended up kissing you good-night. And God only knows what would have happened next."

She swallowed. He hadn't kissed her then. But she was pretty sure he was going to kiss her now. And she wanted him to.

In fact she wanted him so badly right now it seemed as if nothing else really signified. She could remember how it had felt to be in his arms, and she wanted that sensation again. And more.

She wanted him to kiss her the way a real man would kiss a woman. As if he meant it. As if he were claiming her for all time.

Chapter Eight

But Farley didn't move any closer. And he made no move to kiss her, either.

Instead he handed Cassidy the reins to Lucy, which he'd been holding with his other hand.

She stared at him for a moment, confused. What had this been about? Was he toying with her? Or had he just told her that the age gap between them had been too big before and still was today?

"Is this about getting even with me?" she finally asked.

"What the hell does that mean?"

"It means you were going to kiss me. Then you backed off. Like you're trying to teach me a lesson or something."

He looked exasperated. "You're the one who just told me how desperately you want to work in Billings. Explain to me why it would make any sense at all for me to kiss you."

"Then why did you look like you wanted to?"

"Lord, woman, you're going to drive me crazy. For the record, I'm not the kind of guy who plays games when it comes to love. Teaching you some kind of 'lesson' was the last thing on my mind."

"Well, then." She put her hands on her hips, not ready to let this go. "What *was* on your mind, then?"

"Four years ago it seemed like you'd changed into a different sort of person. I guess today I was thinking you hadn't changed as much as I'd thought you had."

"And is that a good thing?"

"Damn it, Cassidy, I don't want to discuss this anymore. You've got your life plan and I've got mine. Let's leave it at that. And now can we please make tracks?"

He was already astride Chickweed by the time she recovered her senses enough to mount Lucy and follow his lead across the creek back onto Coffee Creek land.

They didn't push their horses, but they didn't dawdle, either. They made up time by cutting through to an access road and taking a more direct route back to the ranch.

Suddenly it was all business between them, which left Cassidy disconcerted, but also—*face it*—relieved. Kissing Farley would have been such a huge mistake. Thank goodness he'd been smart enough not to go there.

And now that they were back at the barn, she felt guilty for ever having left. Finnegan didn't even twitch an ear when she went to say hello to him. She noticed he'd drunk some of his water but hadn't touched his feed.

Though they'd taken Lucy and Chickweed a lot farther than they'd intended, both horses seemed better for the fresh air and exercise. Still, Farley wouldn't let them out with the other horses until they'd been tested and found clear of infection.

"They should have absolutely no contact with Finnegan, or anything he touches. Unfortunately, not all horses who've had strangles develop an immunity to it."

Cassidy groaned. So now she had to keep two areas

separate within the barn. One for recovering horses and one for horses still battling the infection.

"I know it's more work, but the cleaner you keep things, the sooner this will be all behind you."

Cassidy settled Lucy and Chickweed in fresh stalls, then went to check on Finnegan again. Farley was just finishing up his examination.

She slipped into the other side of the stall and laid her face against Finnegan's dear neck. "You need to eat, sweetie." She looked over at Farley. "There has to be something more we can do."

She was consumed with guilt for having taken off this afternoon, while poor Finnegan suffered all on his own.

"I'm sorry. At this point all we can do is try to keep him comfortable. Anti-inflammatory drugs and penicillin is what we've got. You can try hot compresses, but I don't think they'll be as effective with him as they were with the others."

CASSIDY CARRIED FARLEY'S grim words in with her that evening as she joined her mother at the dinner table. "Lucy and Chickweed are almost completely recovered, but Finnegan isn't getting any better. Farley says there's not much more we can do for him."

"Given Finnegan's age, I'm not surprised."

That struck Cassidy as a little harsh, but then her mother had never been sentimental about any of their animals—certainly not Sky, whom she'd tried to ban from the house, until Cassidy wore her out after years of sneaking her into her room to sleep every night.

No, her mother saved all her maternal instincts for her children, and Cassidy supposed she shouldn't fault her for that.

"I've been thinking about Winnie and the baby," Olive said, between bites of her salad. "I've decided to send Winnie a note. I won't mention the baby. I'll just say that I hope she is doing better and hope to see her back in Coffee Creek one day."

Cassidy was surprised at her mother's restraint. "That sounds like a smart plan." She waited a beat then asked, "Any calls for me today?" She already checked for messages. There weren't any.

"Not that I noticed. But I wasn't around much. The meeting took most of my afternoon."

Anxious to avoid that subject, Cassidy jumped into another topic. "Farley and I took Lucy and Chickweed out for a little exercise. They seemed good as new."

"You and Farley? That's nice." Olive smiled at her approvingly. "He's a good man. Did you know his land abuts ours for about a mile on our western boundary?"

"I had no idea. I didn't even realize he owned much land." She'd never been on Farley's property, except when she'd taken Sky for her vaccines to the clinic which was next to the ranch house.

"Oh, yes. The Farleys were big-time ranchers back in the day. Over the years they've sold a lot of their land, but they still own about a thousand acres." Her mother removed their salad plates and returned with bowls of southwestern-style chicken chili. "So where did you go for your ride?"

"Farther than we intended." Cassidy reached for her spoon enthusiastically. "Did the housekeeper make this?"

"Bonny? Yes. She made cookies, too, if you have any room."

Cassidy took a taste and made a note to thank Bonny the next time she saw her.

"You and Farley must have had fun," her mother said. "You were gone for quite a long time."

"The horses needed exercise." She had a feeling her mother's matchmaking instincts were on alert and didn't want to feed that any more than she had to. "Before we knew it, we'd reached Silver Creek. Remember the old barn that almost burned down sixteen years ago? It's still standing, though only barely."

The light drained from her mother's eyes, and her smile vanished, leaving traces of fine lines branching out from her puckered lips. "That place should be razed."

Cassidy had never thought of her mother as old. She had far too much vitality for that. Yet, now she could see that the passing years were taking their toll. Her mother may not be old, but she *was* aging. And clearly she *did not* want to talk about the events of sixteen years ago.

"Eat your chili, Cassidy. It's getting cold."

THE NEXT MORNING a low front moved over central Montana and Cassidy woke up to a heavy, gray sky with the scent of rain on the wind.

Her mother had convinced her to sleep in the house for a change, but first thing, even before brushing her teeth, she pulled on her jeans and a flannel shirt, and went out to check the horses. Sky wanted to come with her, but she convinced her dog to stay inside where it was nice and dry.

It had rained some in the night. The gravel paths were slick and the trees and grasses glistened with fresh moisture. She studied the sky and figured it would likely be raining off-and-on all day.

Rather than head back for a rain slicker, she dashed

to the barn where she found everyone in pretty much the same shape as she'd left them the day before.

Lucy and Chickweed chowed down their breakfasts and swished their tails impatiently as she cleaned their stalls.

"I know you want to be out with the others, but trust me. Today you should be happy to be inside."

Finnegan was the same. No better, but hopefully no worse, either. She brushed him down gently, more to give her an excuse to spend time with him than anything else. She put on fresh hot compresses and changed out his water and his feed, hoping something fresh might entice his appetite.

But he just looked at her with listless eyes.

"Oh, sweetie, don't give up. You have to fight this thing, okay?"

Finnegan shuffled his feet.

"That a boy," she encouraged, holding a handful of warm mush to his mouth.

He took a taste, then changed his mind and averted his head, just like a toddler refusing a nasty spoonful of vegetables.

"Oh, Finnegan." She didn't know what to do. She really didn't.

THE REST OF that week passed in much the same way. Lots of rain, lots of mud and an endless routine of disinfecting, nursing, hoping and praying.

Meanwhile, in the main house the painters came—and went.

The antique armoire was delivered and the old desk removed.

On Wednesday Olive went to town and returned with

the finished duvet, cushion covers and a new set of drapes, which Cassidy helped her hang.

When they were done, Olive surveyed the room with satisfaction. "Good. That's one job done."

Cassidy didn't dare say that she'd liked the room better the old way. Knowing that her mother was waiting for a reaction, she forced a smile. "It's beautiful, Mom. Like a posh hotel room. Thanks."

"My pleasure, Cassidy. I'm just glad you like it." Her mom patted her hand, then left the room.

AFTER A WEEK of rain, the air was muggy and close in the barn, yet Cassidy went back to sleeping on the cot in order to be close to Finnegan. As her mother packed for an overnight trip to Billings to look at some stock, Olive rolled her eyes and declared that Cassidy's devotion to Finnegan was overkill.

"You have to remember, he's just a horse. When I asked you to take care of this outbreak, I never expected you to provide 24/7 service. You'll wear yourself out at this rate."

It wasn't that Cassidy enjoyed sleeping on the cot.

If Finnegan had shown even the slightest degree of improvement, she would have been glad to spend a night in her newly jazzed-up bedroom.

But Finnegan still wasn't eating. And he'd lost a significant amount of weight thanks to the strangles. Running her hand over the horse's belly that evening, Cassidy could count his ribs.

"Oh, I wish you'd eat. Just a little."

But Finnegan refused even water this evening. Another very bad sign.

Cassidy was sitting on the edge of her cot, wondering if she should call Farley, when she heard footsteps crunching on gravel, then the barn door rolling open.

In came Corb. He had a thermos and a paper bag in hand.

"Laurel noticed the light was on out here again. Seems like you're spending a lot of nights in the barn these days, Cass."

"I feel better when I'm close to him."

"You better be careful you don't make yourself sick." He handed her the thermos and bag.

Cassidy checked them out. Hot coffee and a chicken sandwich. "Yum. Thank Laurel for me, okay?"

"Will do." He started to leave, then hesitated. "You know it doesn't help anything, you sleeping out here."

"Maybe. But I couldn't stand it if I woke up one morning and came out here to find—" She couldn't say the rest without giving in to tears. Finnegan had been a good, loyal horse and there was no way she was going to leave him to die alone. No way.

Not that she'd written him off, the way she could tell her mother—and even Corb—had done.

They didn't understand what a proud spirit her horse had. He could beat this. He *would* beat this.

Corb sighed and shook his head. "How about I stay here tonight and you sleep in the house?"

"Thanks, but no. This is my job and Finnegan is my horse. Besides, you have a wife and a baby who need you."

He chuckled drily. "Now that you mention it, I might get more rest out here than I do in there."

"Maybe so. But I need to be here."

"Stubborn girl." He laid a hand on the top of her head, a rare gesture of affection. "I guess I'll see you in the morning, then."

"Good night, Corb. Thanks again for the food." The sandwich was delicious and there was a note at the bottom of the bag explaining that the coffee was decaf so she shouldn't be nervous to drink it all.

Cassidy had to admit that the hot, flavorful coffee went down nicely with her sandwich.

She was just pouring herself a second cupful when she noticed two things. A slight breeze cooling her neck. And Sky was no longer lounging by her cot.

She jumped to her feet, right away noticing that Corb had left the barn door ajar. Had Sky slipped out?

And then Cassidy heard an awful growl, then barking and a cry of pain.

CASSIDY GRABBED A pitchfork and ran out the open door, triggering the motion detector lights as she raced into the yard, then around to the pasture, following the terrible sounds of canine growling and yelping.

She was out of range of the floodlights now, tripping over the uneven ground as she ran. The full moon was low, casting an eerie orange glow over the field. A flash of movement caught her eye, and then she saw them, the coyote circling Sky, about to make a second attack. Sky, obviously wounded, was a sitting duck.

"Get out of here, you awful thing!" Cassidy charged with the pitchfork and only then did the coyote start to slink away. But not after at least one yearning look at the prey he'd almost felled.

"Oh, Sky! Are you all right?"

Sky's soft whimper was truly pathetic. Cassidy dropped the pitchfork and tenderly caressed her dog. As she touched the fur around her neck, she felt a slick of something warm and wet.

The smell of blood on her hand was unmistakable.

"Oh, Sky, how badly did he hurt you?" She gathered the dog in her arms. Cassidy could haul a thirty-pound bag of feed without too much trouble. She could damn well carry her dog, too, if she had to.

But where should she go? What should she do?

Cassidy moved as fast as her shaking legs would carry her. Her mother was in Billings—should she call Corb?

No. The answer came to her in a flash of certainty.

She had to take Sky to Farley. He was only a fifteen-minute drive away.

The walk to her truck seemed to take forever. Trying not to cry, she murmured comforting words to her dog. "It's okay. Farley will fix you."

But what if Farley couldn't? It would be more than she could stand to lose her dog in this awful way. That damn coyote. And her, too, for not noticing Corb hadn't closed the door all the way.

Cassidy settled Sky in the foot well of the passenger side, then grabbed the blanket she kept in her truck for emergencies and wrapped it around her dog.

As she reached for the keys she'd left dangling in the ignition—a lazy habit of hers when she was out on the ranch—she realized her fingers were slick with blood. She wiped them clean on her jeans, then started driving.

She went as fast as she dared, all too aware of the potential hazard of wildlife crossing the road. She could do nothing to stop her tears, but she opened her window so the wind and cool air would clear her head.

A phone call warning Farley of her arrival would be a good idea.

But she didn't dare reach for the mobile phone in her pocket.

She supposed this wouldn't be the first time the vet had been woken from his sleep by a distraught rancher.

FARLEY WASN'T HAVING a good night. He'd finally found the time to go out for dinner with Amber this evening. When he'd dropped her home, he'd told her that he appreciated how patient she'd been with him, but he didn't think their relationship was going to work out.

"That's okay," she'd said.

She hadn't pressed him for details, not that he would have given any if she had.

How could he tell Amber that it was another woman who put him in a fever whenever he was around her? Cassidy Lambert. If it wasn't for that damn case of strangles she might have come and gone from Coffee Creek without him even knowing about it.

That would have been better.

Maybe then his relationship with Amber would have stood a chance…

But now Cassidy was in his head again. In his thoughts during the day and his dreams at night.

He couldn't stop thinking about her. Wanting her. Cursing himself for not kissing her when he'd had the chance. So what if he couldn't have her forever? Right now one night seemed like it would be enough.

Really? Just one night? Is that the kind of man you are now?

His sheets were tangled from all his tossing and turning, and a fine sweat had broken out over his skin. When the sound of a vehicle pulling into his yard carried through his open window, at first he thought he had to be hearing things.

But there was no mistaking the heavy knocking at his door.

And then a voice, crying out for help.

"Farley. Please, Farley! You have to help."

Good God, it was Cassidy. What had happened?

He was out of bed and into his jeans and T-shirt in less than five seconds. Down the hall and to the door in five seconds more. He twisted the lock and pulled on the handle. And in stumbled Cassidy, with Sky in her arms and blood everywhere.

She'd been crying and her hair was windblown and wild.

"What happened?"

"Sky was attacked by a coyote. Right outside the home barn. Oh, Farley, she's lost a lot of blood."

He'd already slipped on his boots. Now he gently eased Sky out of her arms. "Follow me. We'll go to the clinic and get a proper look at her."

The motion-detector lights flicked on as they hurried along the stone path that led to his office. He always locked up at night, protecting the expensive equipment and drugs that might be the target of thieves. But the keys were still in his jeans and he shifted Sky's weight to his left arm so he could pull them out.

He shouldered the door open, then flipped the light switch. In the sudden bright halogen glare he could see that Cassidy was drawn and pale. She blinked at the onslaught of so much light, then she shuddered. "The blood. It's everywhere…"

She was sounding like Lady Macbeth now, and he was worried.

But then she'd told him, hadn't she? *I'm terrible with blood…*

"Sit down, Cass. Now. Before you faint." He placed Sky gently on the aluminum examining table that Liz would have disinfected before she went home this evening. Sky, poor thing, was shaking. Though she didn't fight Farley, it was Cassidy she kept her gaze trained on.

And Cassidy, who had done as he'd asked and collapsed into the chair by the table, reached out a hand to her dog. "It's okay, Sky. You're going to be okay."

Though her voice was reassuring, there was fear in her eyes when she looked at Farley. Now that she'd accomplished her mission and delivered her dog to help, Cassidy's tears started again. He could see them welling up, then overflowing to her cheekbones, where they hovered for several seconds before spilling down to her jaw. He wanted—badly—to comfort her.

But first he had to see if he could save her dog.

He found the source of the bleeding, parted the border collie's long hair and examined the gaping wound.

As was to be expected, the coyote had gone for Sky's neck, and had managed to make a good-sized gash.

But it wasn't too deep, thankfully. "We'll clean this up, then a few stitches will patch this nicely."

"So she's going to live?"

"The injury isn't life-threatening," he was happy to reassure her. He gave Sky a quick once-over but found no other obvious signs of trauma. "We'll booster her rabies vaccine just to be sure, but it seems she came out of that fight okay. Strange that the coyote went after a dog this size."

As he reached for his supplies, he glanced at Cassidy. "Tell me what happened."

She explained how Corb had brought her out a sandwich and coffee, then left the door ajar.

"As soon as I realized Sky wasn't in the barn anymore, I jumped up to look for her. And at that exact moment, Sky barked and I heard growling and snarling."

She shivered. "So I grabbed a pitchfork and chased off the coyote. But I was too late."

"Actually, you probably saved her life." Farley wasn't at all surprised that Cassidy would be prepared to jump into battle against the coyote to save Sky's life. If the attacker had been a wolf, or even a bear, he knew she would have done the exact same thing. "Sky's older now. Slower and weaker. I guess the coyote figured he could take her."

Fifteen minutes later, Sky was all cleaned and stitched up. He'd had to shave some hair around her wound, so she looked bedraggled.

Not unlike her owner.

Cassidy rose shakily from her seat. "Thanks so much. You'll be mighty tired tomorrow—I'm sorry about that."

As if he cared. He liked the fact that Cassidy had come running to him when she needed help—even if it was just his vet skills she'd wanted.

She assessed Sky doubtfully. "Will it hurt her if I pick her up?"

"Let me." Carefully he scooped the border collie into his arms. Sky barely whimpered.

Cassidy opened the door for him and locked up behind them. As he started on the path back to the house, he heard her behind him.

"Farley? Where are you going? My truck's over here."

"I know where your truck is."

"But it's late. You need some sleep and I should get home and check on Finnegan."

"Has his condition worsened since I saw him last?"

"About the same, I'd say."

"Then he'll be fine until morning."

"That's what Mom and Corb said. It's easier to believe coming from you. So you think he's getting better?"

She looked so hopeful he hated to reply with the truth. "I can't promise that. But he has some time left. And maybe he'll rally."

She pressed her lips together with fresh determination. "Then I have to go."

He studied her pale face, bloodstained hands and clothing, and sagging posture. It would be better for both of them if he let her do just that. But the Lambert family had already suffered a tragic loss due to a car crash. So he pointed out the obvious. "You're in no condition to drive."

"But—"

"Get your ass in the house, Cassidy." He tipped his head toward Sky. "Don't forget—I have a hostage."

Chapter Nine

The man was wonderful—he'd saved her dog—but also infuriating. His attitude right now reminded her of his reaction that night four years ago, when he'd insisted that since he'd driven her to the dance, he was damn well driving her home, as well.

She wanted to argue.

But she was too tired.

She also couldn't deny the flood of gratitude she was feeling toward him right now.

She couldn't have stood it if Sky hadn't been okay. To lose her beloved pet of fourteen years in such a bloody and violent way would have been too cruel. It was bad enough that Sky had been hurt and traumatized.

So she fell in behind Farley as he led her around the side of the house. When he paused at the door, she hurried ahead to open it for him, but though Sky was pretty heavy, he still waited for her to enter first.

On her previous visits to Farley's place she'd never seen anything other than his main foyer and the clinic. This first glimpse of his private space impressed her. The large mudroom had tiled floors, stainless steel countertops, a laundry area and a huge closet. It was practical, but also beautiful, with a calm color scheme and some humorous prints of farm animals, including one with a bird on a cow's head.

The clicking of nails on tile announced the arrival of Farley's own two dogs.

Cassidy had met Tom and Dick before and she had a chance to say hello to each of them, before Farley ordered them out of the room.

"You can shower in there." He pointed to a room next to the closet. "A clean robe is on the hook. Use that while I throw your jeans and shirt into the wash. Just hand them out the door."

She shook her head. "I'll shower when I get home."

For an answer, he just pointed at the mirror over the laundry tub sink. She stared at herself for several long seconds before silently going into the bathroom.

Here, again, she was impressed. The place was spotless, modern and almost spalike. The sink was long—like a trough—and the shower was the kind with a half-dozen different body spray heads as well as an overhead rain shower nozzle.

Quickly she stripped and passed out her jeans and T-shirt. The harsh iron smell of blood was deep in her lungs. She thought she'd never be rid of it.

But the mint-scented shampoo helped. So did the massaging jets of warm water. Worried that she was going to empty Farley's hot water tank, she finally forced herself to turn off the taps after fifteen minutes.

There had been no conditioner for her hair, so brushing it out would have been impossible, even if Farley had owned a comb up to the job. His own little brush, set neatly to the side of the sink, would snap in two if she tried to run it through all these snarls.

Still, she was clean.

She slipped into the white robe, disregarding the slippers that were lined up beneath them. They were much too big, and anyway, she was toasty warm after that great shower.

She walked past the churning washing machine into a kitchen that took her breath away. Lights over the stove and recessed around the moldings showcased French Country white cabinets and vintage-looking Heartland appliances.

The kitchen was divided from the family room by a large island and on the other side she saw Farley by a beautiful river-rock fireplace, adding a log to a couple that were already snapping. And right next to the hearth, Sky was settled in as cozy as could be, with Farley's dogs a polite distance away.

There was even soft music playing. And a pot of tea and cookies on the massive wood coffee table.

"Wow. This place is pretty gorgeous."

At the sound of her voice, Sky raised her head, but was too weak, or perhaps too traumatized, to leave the blanket Farley had placed for her by the heat of the fire.

"I did some renovations a few years ago," Farley said as if they had been nothing significant.

"I'll say." She glanced around, noticing the art on the walls, the well-placed area rugs, lamps and an outstanding bronze of a cowboy wrestling a steer on the table behind the sofa.

All the little touches that men weren't supposed to bother with.

"Did someone help you?"

"Like a designer, you mean?"

Actually, she'd been thinking of a girlfriend. But she nodded.

"Not really. The people at the furniture and paint

stores offered suggestions. But I had an idea what I wanted."

The way he looked at her when he said that last bit made her very aware of her naked skin beneath the smooth cotton of the robe. Yes, Farley was the sort of person who knew what he wanted.

And what he didn't. The snub he'd given her this afternoon when they were out riding still burned, even though she knew she wasn't being logical.

She didn't want Farley. She wanted the job in Billings. And to give a more serious relationship with Josh a shot.

The strangles infection had sidelined her for a few weeks. That was why she hadn't thought much about Josh since she'd arrived and been too busy to answer his calls and text messages.

Is that really true?

Or is the plain truth that Josh can't stack up next to a man like Farley?

The vet had changed into a clean T-shirt and jeans while she'd been showering. The clothes weren't tight, but they couldn't hide his strong muscular build. His dark hair gleamed and so did his eyes, set off to perfection by those sharp cheekbones.

Everything he was she could see in his face. Proud. Powerful. Most intimidating of all…perceptive.

"Don't be scared. This isn't some grand seduction plan."

"I wasn't thinking that," she said quickly.

She went to sit on the hearth, carefully wrapping the robe around her legs so just her ankles and bare feet were peeking out. She placed a light hand on Sky's back, and her dog relaxed back to sleep.

He could *say* he had no plans to seduce her. But she'd

have to be blind not to see the heat in his eyes. Just like she'd seen it earlier when they were at Silver Creek.

"Have some tea and a cookie," he suggested. "Sugar is good after a shock."

Her mind flashed back to the terrible fight between Sky and the coyote. The raw, desperate noises. The smell of the blood. Sky's limp body and her pleading eyes.

She moved forward to the floor, settling in front of the spread he'd laid out, and took a bite of the oatmeal chocolate chip cookies. They weren't the kind from a package.

"Don't tell me you bake as well as excel in interior design?"

A corner of his mouth turned up. "Those are from Liz. Have I ever told you that she manages my life?"

"Right down to baking cookies. That's some assistant you have. I'd keep her, if I was you." She poured some tea for herself and when she looked at Farley and he nodded, she filled his mug, too.

"It's why I put up with her meddling. She's the one who set me up with Amber."

Cassidy had been lifting the mug to her mouth when he said this. She paused...*steady now*...then sipped. "And how is that working out?"

"Not as good as Liz hoped. Amber's lovely. But she lives a forty-five-minute drive from here and I don't have much free time."

A forty-five-minute drive wasn't that bad. Not in Montana.

"You're going to have slim pickings if you're looking for a single woman who lives closer than that."

She polished off the rest of the cookie, not daring to meet his gaze. *Her* ranch was fifteen minutes from his, but that meant nothing. First of all, she wasn't going to be living there much longer. And secondly, he hadn't really broken up with Amber because of the distance between them. If he'd really liked her, he would be willing to drive double that far to see her.

"Maybe I'm not looking. Period. Me and the dogs, we're pretty comfortable the way we are."

"No one you can count on more than your dog," she agreed. She reached across the table again. "These are so good I'm going to have another."

"Please do. And take a seat, would you? Your legs have to be cramping down there."

"I should go home."

"You don't have any clothes," he said calmly.

Right. She felt such a fool. Awkwardly she made her way to the sofa, settling on the far cushion, then leaning back into the softly plumped, leather-covered seat.

The sound of a buzzer startled her but with his same steady calm, Farley got to his feet. "Sounds like the wash cycle is finished. I'll throw your things into the dryer. Is that okay?"

"Sure. Thanks."

While he was gone, she gave the room a closer look. There were photos of his parents on a built-in shelving unit. Also a picture of him graduating from college and another with him and the dogs.

On the lower shelf she found a chessboard with pieces carved from jade. By the time he returned from the laundry, she had a game set up on the table.

"Do you play?" she asked. Her father had taught her and her brothers during the long, cold winters of their childhood. Corb and Brock had never enjoyed it much, but she and B.J. had both been keen.

"I used to. With my dad."

"Me, too. And since we have time to kill before the clothes dry…"

If he realized she was using the game as a safety barrier between them, he gave no sign of it.

"Okay. Let's do it. You can be white."

Cassidy started with a classic opening, placing her center pawn two squares forward.

Farley countered with a similar move. "So you asked about my love life. It's only fair I get to ask about yours."

"Hmm?" She moved her next pawn forward one space.

"Corb tells me there's a guy in your life. Josh."

She frowned. "Corb shouldn't talk about things he doesn't know about." She'd never mentioned Josh to her mother or her brothers. They only knew about him because he'd phoned the house number a few times—despite her request that he only call her on her mobile phone.

"So you're not serious?"

No question that Josh wanted them to be. "I'm not sure."

Farley moved his next pawn and she countered with a move from her rook.

"Interesting," he said.

"What? My relationship with Josh? Or the move I just made in chess?"

His hand hovered over the board as he contemplated his next play. Her gaze lingered on his hands. They were strong, yes. But they also had a long-fingered grace. As a vet he needed both qualities to meet the demands of a job that required him to handle six-hundred-pound cows and horses and yet also perform delicate surgical procedures.

"I'm just saying, it's interesting. You tell me you're

a free woman, and I'm a free man. Just because I didn't kiss you this afternoon didn't mean I didn't want to."

Cassidy narrowed her eyes. He was making moves here that had nothing to do with chess pieces. "You said this wasn't a seduction scene."

If it had been, that would have scared her off. Right? Then why didn't she feel scared *now?*

"I said I wasn't *planning* a seduction. If you decide you'd like to make love, though, I wouldn't say no."

Just hearing him say those words started her pulse racing. "Like I'd do that."

"Agreed, it's a long shot." Still, he reached for her hand. And she let him have it.

"Besides, you aren't looking for a woman in your life."

"I wasn't talking about a lifetime. As I understand it, that isn't what you have to offer, either."

She ought to be shocked at his suggestion that they have a one-night stand. But the way he was touching her hand, running his thumb in slow circles on her palm, was so hypnotizing.

"That's pretty scandalous, Dan Farley."

Was that really her, sounding so bold? But she *felt* bold. That was the thing. So strange and unlike her. With her eyes she willed him to come closer and when he placed a hand on her shoulder, she touched him, too.

She could see his eyes so clearly now, and what she saw thrilled her. A dark, pulsing energy was swirling around them, blocking out the world.

But all the anticipation was nothing compared to how she felt when he actually lowered his lips to hers. His kiss unleashed something inside of her, a power and a desperate need that she hadn't even realized she possessed.

Oh, Farley! She tangled her fingers in his hair as their kiss deepened. His arms banded around her waist, pulling her closer, and the contact with his solid, heated chest only heightened her pleasure and her desire… for *more*.

But just as she was ready to slip her robe off her shoulders out of an aching need to have him touch her more intimately, a buzzer sounded from the mudroom again.

The dryer.

Damn, awful timing.

Farley's kisses began to gentle. He pressed his lips to her cheek, to the corner of her eyes, then the top of her head.

She struggled to understand. He'd started this. Why was he stopping?

She tried to find the answer in his eyes, but he had them closed. She watched as he swallowed. Then took a deep breath.

"Cass. Honey. It's time you went home."

"You're serious? What was this that just happened?"

"You have to admit it was more fun than chess." He touched the side of her face gently, then stood. "Let's see if your jeans are dry."

SHE'D NEVER MET a more infuriating man. It was the middle of the night and Cassidy was driving slowly, out of consideration for Sky's injuries, wanting to keep any jostling to a minimum.

So she vented her frustration by pounding her palms on the steering wheel.

He'd kissed her because he'd found the chess game boring.

Really?

So all those sparks—all that sexual tension—that had been in her mind only?

She didn't believe it.

But what if it were true? Maybe he'd just wanted to humiliate her the way she'd embarrassed him that night at the Harvest Dance. Because she'd been ready to strip off her robe and make love with him. And he'd turned her away.

As it had turned out, her jeans were still damp, but she'd put them on without complaint. Farley had walked her to the truck, but only so he could help settle Sky in for the drive home.

"Thanks again for fixing my dog," she'd said stiffly, as she climbed into the driver's seat.

There wasn't enough light to see any expression in his eyes as she drove away. Maybe there hadn't been any expression worth seeing.

FARLEY STOOD IN the driveway long past the time that Cassidy's taillights had disappeared from view. The cool air helped bring his libido back under control. If he hadn't put a halt to it, they could have been making love right now.

But he'd put on the brakes. He didn't know if he'd just done the smartest thing in his life. Or the stupidest.

With eerie timing, a marauding gang of coyotes let out a series of yips that echoed in the hollow where his great-grandfather had built their home. For all Farley knew one of them had been Sky's attacker, and yet he couldn't feel any animosity toward the animals.

In fact, he felt a certain kinship. He couldn't deny he had an urge of his own to howl at the moon tonight.

At least she was no longer scared of him. If anything, she'd discovered her own power. Maybe now he should be scared of her.

EXHAUSTION HAD SET in by the time Cassidy reached Coffee Creek Ranch. After checking Finnegan and finding him holding his own, she decided to take everyone's advice and finish out the night in her own bed, with Sky sleeping at her feet as usual.

The unfamiliar bedding, the dark shadow of the new armoire against the far wall and the smell of fresh paint were useful for one thing—distracting her from thoughts of Farley.

Her utter tiredness helped, too. She closed her eyes and the next thing she knew the sun was rising, blanketing the horizon with a wash of fresh orange light.

She convinced Sky to stay inside when she went out to do her chores. The storm system had finally passed on, and the day was breaking clear and bright. She took it as another good sign when she was able to convince Finnegan to eat some mush straight from her hand. She was burning his bedding in an area set off from the barns and pastures when she saw Jackson drive up to the equine barn.

He'd either been up awfully early this morning, or he had spent the night away. Could it be a woman?

Somehow she didn't think so. Jackson looked so morose these days—not at all like a man who was enjoying the excitement of a new relationship. Or even the comfort of an older one.

Once she'd extinguished the fire, she decided to see if he would talk to her.

The equine barn was double the size of the one they used for their home horses. Olive had spared no expense in the design or outfitting. She wanted potential buyers to be impressed when they came to check out their herd.

And she'd been even more careful in selecting the breeding stock for the operation. The result was that Coffee Creek Ranch now had the reputation for breeding some of the finest American quarter horses in Montana.

Cassidy found Jackson giving orders to a couple of the hired men. They were monitoring several mares, trying to pick the optimum time for breeding. She waited until they were finished their discussion and asked him how he was doing.

"Fine." He paused, then nodded toward the door. "Want to go for a walk?"

"Sure." She followed him back into the sunshine and out to the pasture where the mares were grazing. She noticed the spring growth had been picked over pretty well, and Jackson must have been thinking the same thing.

"We need to move them out soon, now that the warmer weather seems to be settling in."

Cassidy eyed the herd, looking to see if any of the horses seemed dispirited or uninterested in grazing. "They all seem healthy."

"Yeah. You've done a good job of keeping the infection contained."

A compliment from her foster brother—always a man of few words—was something to be savored. "Thank you."

"You put your heart and soul into it. The way you tackle everything you do." He gave her a little smile. "But you didn't come to me to talk about the strangles, did you?"

Cassidy knew she had to choose her words carefully.

Jackson was a grown man with every right to come and go as he pleased without a family inquisition. "I don't mean to pry. I just want to know if everything's okay."

"That's a tough one. Do I still miss Brock each and every day? Yes, I do. But I'm sure all you do, too. What you don't have to feel every day is the responsibility of knowing you contributed to his death."

"That's harsh, Jackson. And totally unfair. If a bolt of lightning had struck the truck, would you have blamed yourself for that, too?"

Jackson's eyes flickered, but he didn't respond. Cassidy sighed out of frustration. "Is that why you were out last night? Did it have something to do with Brock?"

"In a way." He studied her face for a bit, as if weighing consequences in his mind. Then he seemed to come to a conclusion. Placing a hand on her shoulder he said, "You know Brock used to go over to Silver Creek Ranch and help out your aunt now and then."

"Yes. I heard about that."

"He thought it was totally bogus the way the family had cut her off."

"It never felt right," Cassidy agreed. "But there must be reasons."

"According to Corb, Maddie didn't tell your mother when their father had his stroke. Your mother won't forgive Maddie for denying her the chance to say her farewells before he died."

"That's awful!" Cassidy knew she'd always treasure her own last moments with her father. He'd had his first heart attack in the morning, been rushed to the hospital in Great Falls, then passed away two days later. Her mother had been by his side the entire time and Cassidy and her brothers had all had a chance to see him, too. "Did Brock know that?"

"I don't think so. But I suspect he would have said that there are always two sides to a story. Since he passed on, I've felt it was my duty to continue where he left off and help Maddie whenever I have free time. That's where I was last night—working until dark re-shingling her roof. She invited me to bunk over and I couldn't say no. I could tell she wasn't feeling well and didn't want to be alone."

Cassidy didn't know what to think. She felt sorry for her aunt, but she still wanted to know why Maddie hadn't told Olive when their father had that stroke. Why would anyone deny someone the chance to say farewell to their beloved parent?

"Do you think Mom knew what Brock was up to?"

"No, but your father did."

"Really?"

"Yup. Though his loyalty to your mother made it impossible for him to say so, I think he approved."

Cassidy didn't doubt that. Her father had been such a softie. "Jackson, I feel awful about Maddie Turner. Is there anything I should do?"

"Just stay out of it, Cassidy. It's better if you don't get involved." He glanced back at the barn. She could tell he didn't want to discuss the topic any further.

She sighed. Why was life always so complicated?

"I should go check on Sky. She had a tussle with a coyote last night and I had to take her to Farley's for some stitches." She made a show of scraping some mud off her boot as she said this, in case her expression gave anything away.

"That explains your hair, I guess."

Cassidy put a hand to her head. She'd forgotten that she still hadn't brushed out all the tangles. "I was covered in blood. Farley made me shower at his place, but he didn't have any conditioner."

"Is that a fact." Jackson looked amused. But only for a moment. "I'm sorry I wasn't home to help you last night. Damn, those coyotes are getting pretty brash if they'll come right up to the yard."

"Maybe it was the full moon." It might explain more than the coyotes' behavior.

Chapter Ten

After breakfast, Cassidy decided that Lucy and Chickweed needed some fresh air and exercise. She took Lucy first, into one of the training pens. On a lark, she rolled out three barrels and made a makeshift barrel racing track.

"Ever seen one of these before?" she asked Lucy. "I have a feeling you're going to find this really fun." She tacked up the horse, then walked her through the circuit, letting Lucy familiarize herself with the wooden barrels.

At the first barrel Lucy paused and blew air from her nostrils, and then she grew more frisky, as if she sensed that a game was in the offing and she was anxious to get going.

Lucy seemed like a natural as she traced the distinctive cloverleaf pattern around the barrels. And she instinctively made tight, clean turns around each one.

After just their second trial circuit, Lucy tossed her head and gave a snort as if to say, *I get it. Can we do it faster now?*

So Cassidy urged her back to the imaginary start line. She held her in place for about thirty seconds, then let loose with a holler.

"Yeah! Go, Lucy, go!"

Cassidy laughed as her horse took off, following the path that they'd been tracing earlier, only much faster. She nicked the first barrel and totally trashed the second, but sailed around the third with no incident.

"Not bad. Not bad at all."

Cassidy hadn't realized she had an audience. Suddenly self-conscious, she trotted Lucy to the fence. Farley had his arms resting on the top rung, a big smile on his face.

"Decided to train her to be a barrel racer after all, huh?"

She shook her head. "Just having some fun."

His gaze swept over her, and self-consciously she put a hand to her hair, wishing she'd remembered to put on a hat, or at least pulled the mess into a ponytail or something.

Farley didn't seem any worse for the excitement of the previous night. He looked as strong, calm and unflappable as ever.

"How was Sky this morning?"

"Tired, but good. She ate a little breakfast and had a lot of water." Heat was rising up her neck to her face. It had nothing to do with the exertion of the ride and everything to do with seeing Farley.

Would he mention the kiss?

"That's a good sign." He broke away from the fence. "Jackson wants me to do some work with his mares this morning. I guess I'd better get started. I heard you laughing, though, and couldn't resist coming to see what you were up to."

He started to walk away, then turned back. "You need to laugh more often. It's a beautiful sound."

By NOON, CASSIDY had finished exercising both Lucy and Chickweed and given them both a thorough grooming. She managed to coax Finnegan into eating a little more mush and dared to hope that before too long her brave, old mustang would be back to normal. When she'd finished scrubbing up, she modified her route back to the house so she could circle around the equine barn and see if Farley's truck was still parked there. It wasn't.

She saw Jackson and Corb, though, mounted on two of the uninfected ranch horses, preparing to move some of the newly pregnant mares to the northwest pasture.

Inside the house, Bonny was washing the kitchen floor on her hands and knees—the way Olive always insisted it had to be done. Cassidy tiptoed around the tiled area on her way to her bedroom.

"Hey, Bonny. Thanks for the chili the other night. It was delicious."

"Glad you liked it." Bonny sat back on her haunches. "Want me to get you some lunch?"

"No thanks. Since Mom still isn't back from her trip, I thought I'd go into town. Do we need anything while I'm there?"

"Not that I can think of." Bonny went back to washing floors and Cassidy took a shower, using copious amounts of conditioner to untangle her hair.

As she grabbed her wallet to leave, Sky gave her a "please stay here and hang out with me" look. But when Cassidy asked if she wanted to go in the truck—a word that usually had Sky bounding to her feet—Sky turned her head and pretended she hadn't heard the offer.

Cassidy cranked up the tunes in her truck as she drove—windows down, her hair blowing. It would be a mess again, but who cared. She was relieved the rain had finally stopped. Sunshine was always good for the spirit. When her phone chimed she decided to pull over and see who was trying to reach her.

Maybe…Farley?

Or the accounting firm?

But no, it was just another text message from Josh, frustrated as usual that she wasn't answering his calls. The disappointment she felt when she saw his name told her something that she'd been suspecting ever since she arrived home.

Had seeing Farley again been part of her change of heart?

In all honesty, she couldn't say no.

But that didn't change the fact that her friendly feelings toward Josh would never reach the level of passion and excitement that she'd felt for Farley last night.

She couldn't tell Josh this by text message. So she called him.

As she waited for him to answer, she prepped a little speech in her head. *This time apart has given me time to think…and I've realized that we're just not right for each other…*

Of course, the actual conversation didn't go quite as smoothly as she'd planned.

"You've been leading me on," Josh complained.

Cassidy decided to take this one on the chin, as her brothers would say. "If I have, then I'm sorry."

"Are you? You don't sound it."

Oh, he sounded like a petulant little boy. "Well, I apologize for that, too. I'm sorry for all of it, Josh, but I hope we can still be friends."

To her surprise, he mumbled, "Maybe." Then hung up.

She took a minute to review the conversation. Had she been cruel? But sometimes that was what honesty required. And she'd been that, at least. If they ended up working at the same accounting firm, she'd just hope that Josh would be decent about it.

By the time she reached the Cinnamon Stick, Cassidy was starving. Eugenia and Laurel were handling the tail end of the luncheon rush. Both booths and all four stools were taken, but that didn't worry her. She'd order a sandwich and eat it outside.

"Where's Steph?" she asked her sister-in-law after ordering the Black Forest sandwich special.

"She's had her lunch and now she's napping." Laurel patted the monitor located on a shelf above the food prep area. "She's usually good for a couple of hours in the afternoon and when she wakes up, she'll have another feeding, then we'll go home." She winked. "That's the plan, anyway."

Eugenia shrugged. "Babies, they have their own ideas about schedules and such. But I must admit, that little Stephanie is one golden child."

"She sure is." Laurel handed Cassidy her sandwich, then in a lower voice said, "Did you know your mother is here?"

Cassidy frowned, then went to the window. Sure enough, parked on the other side of a big horse trailer that had blocked her view was the Coffee Ranch SUV. She scanned the room again.

"Where is she?"

Laurel raised her eyebrows. "In the kitchen. Talking to Vince."

"I didn't think *anyone* talked to Vince."

"Oh, they do. He just doesn't talk back."

Cassidy grinned. "Has she eaten?"

"Not that I know of."

"I'll see if she wants something." Cassidy edged

around the corner, heading for the closed door separating the kitchen from the serving area. She could hear voices, all right. Her mother was speaking.

"—two years and haven't been for dinner once."

"I was there for the baby shower."

"Not the same thing. Why don't you come this Sunday? I'll invite the whole family."

When Vince didn't answer, she added, "Including Jackson."

Why would Vince care if Jackson was invited to dinner or not? Cassidy realized she was eavesdropping, but was too curious to stop.

"I know you mean well. But I'm happy sticking to myself."

"Come on, Vince. We may be old but we're not dead."

Cassidy gasped. Her mother sounded like she was *flirting*. She waited, but again Vince chose to say nothing. She was just about to move before—

And then it was too late. The door swung open and her mother stepped right in front of her.

"Cassidy?"

"I—I came for a sandwich." She held up the paper bag Laurel had given her a minute ago.

"Then what are you doing behind the counter?"

"Laurel told me you were here. I was going to ask if you wanted some lunch, too." But then she'd been distracted by something more interesting than ham and cheese on rye.

"I've eaten, thank you." Her mother sounded distracted. "We've been so busy lately, I was hoping we could all get together for dinner this Sunday. Are you and Corb free?" she asked Laurel.

"We sure are. Can I bring something?"

"Maybe one of Vince's pies for dessert? Unless he decides to bring one himself. I invited him, as well."

"Oh." Laurel paused in the act of wiping clean the counter. "I didn't know you and Vince were friends."

"We went to school together. And yes, we were friends before he got caught up in the rodeo circuit."

The scorn on her mother's face made it clear what she thought about *that* lifestyle. Olive assumed that every cowboy was in it for the partying, the women and the alcohol. She never seemed to see B.J.'s trophies and prize winnings as anything but minor accomplishments at best.

But perhaps it was because she'd seen what the rodeo life had done to Vince that she was so hard on her oldest son, Cassidy reflected.

"Corb and I will try to convince him to come," Laurel promised.

"Good luck with that." From what Cassidy had overheard, she guessed it wasn't going to be easy.

THE NEXT FEW days were hot. Summer had arrived in Montana and with a vengeance.

By Sunday, the humidity had risen to intolerable levels and there was talk of thunderclouds, even though the sky was still clear.

Come three o'clock however, it wasn't. As the clouds gathered, so did the horses, moving into their storm shelters, acting skittish and wild. Cassidy finished her chores early so she could peel potatoes for the dinner and set the table as her mother had asked.

By five-thirty all the family had arrived. Cassidy had commandeered her niece, Corb was opening wine, Jackson was on the patio grilling steaks, Laurel was tossing the salad while Olive checked the potatoes roasting in the oven. Amid all that chaos, the doorbell rang.

"Get that, will you, Cass?" her mother asked.

So her mother had convinced Vince to come after all, Cassidy surmised as she headed for the entrance with Steph tucked snugly in her left arm.

She still thought it was odd that Vince had been invited to a family dinner. She'd asked her mom about it earlier and all Olive had said was that Vince had once been a very dear friend.

"Was he friends with your sister, too?" she'd asked, feeling a little daring for even mentioning Maddie's existence.

"Probably," had been her mom's short answer.

There had to be more to the story, Cassidy thought, remembering the look of pain on Maddie's face that day Vince had said hello to her outside the café.

Maybe she'd find out more about the past tonight.

But when she opened the door it wasn't Vince Butterfield standing on the porch.

Words deserted her.

Finally Farley said, "I guess your mother didn't tell you she'd invited me?"

She shook her head no. Three days had passed since she'd seen him last. But had she thought about him?

Oh, yeah.

"How's Sky doing?"

"So much better. And Finnegan is, too. He's been eating a little more, every day." And then she blurted, "You look good."

He'd dressed up in dark jeans and a Western-style dark shirt, and she thought it would be fair to say she'd never seen a man who looked better in black.

Or sexier.

"You look nice, too. Even combed your hair, I see." He took a strand and let it slide between his fingers, then bent in closer for a look at the baby.

She could smell the botanical mint of his shampoo, and also feel the heat of his body. He touched a finger to Stephanie's cheek and she found herself wishing he would touch her, too.

Heck and darn. Get a grip on yourself.

"Isn't she the sweetest baby?"

"Sure is." But Farley was looking at *her* as he said this.

Gosh, she felt like such a fool. She could feel a flush gathering on her cheeks and she wished her mother had given her some warning.

Though Olive's comment about making an effort with her hair and makeup for a change should have tipped her off.

Farley straightened, and his voice deepened as he said he was glad to hear that Finnegan was eating again. "To be honest, I wasn't sure Finn would be strong enough to beat this thing. I'll come by tomorrow and draw a sample for testing. The sooner we can clear your ranch of the quarantine, the better."

"That would be great." She led the way to the combined kitchen/family room, where Farley was given a warm welcome. His friendship with her brothers was reason enough for him to be here tonight, but Olive's smug smile told Cassidy everything she needed to know about her motives for inviting the vet.

On the pretence of helping her mother with the potatoes, Cassidy passed the baby to Laurel, then went to the stove and murmured, "You can stop with the matchmaking, okay? It isn't going to work."

"Don't be silly. I just wanted to thank Farley for all

the extra work he's been doing for us. I'm so glad that darn strangles didn't spread any further than it did. I have you to thank as well, Cassidy. You did a wonderful job keeping it contained."

Cassidy waited. There was usually a "but" or an "if only" attached to one of her mother's compliments.

"If only you weren't so set on working in the city. You have such a knack with animals."

"I have a knack with numbers, too, Mom. And a good brain. Is it such a crime that I want to use it?"

"Are you saying we don't have to think because we work on a ranch? That we're somehow *inferior* to people who work in offices and ivory towers?"

"Of course that's not what I mean." Cassidy blew out an exasperated breath. Her mother was unbelievably obdurate. How was she ever going to get the message across that she was not going to put up with her mother nosing in on her love life?

When it came time to sit at the table, certain that her mother was going to connive to sit her next to Farley, Cassidy wiggled in for the chair between Jackson and Corb. But in a move worthy of a choreographed ballet, somehow Corb got diverted, Laurel moved over a space, and Farley ended up on her right-hand side after all.

He raised his eyebrows at her and shrugged, as if to say he wasn't sure how it had happened, either.

Cassidy fumed.

It wasn't just her mother. Her whole family was behind this scheme. And she was fed up.

It wasn't that she didn't *want* to sit by Farley. But they made it happen so obviously, it was embarrassing.

Besides, what was Farley to think? That her family thought she was so unappealing they had to find her a man—since she couldn't do it on her own.

Cassidy ate very little of the meal, and added even less to the conversation.

Olive focused most of her efforts on Farley.

"Tell me—you don't have plans to sell any more of your land, do you?"

"No. When Dad retired we let a section go to Cooper Madison. He'd been renting it from us for years and was anxious to own it outright. But we're keeping the rest."

"That's good. You know a corner of your land to the west butts right up to Coffee Creek. It's good grazing."

"I know. Why? Were you interested in renting it?"

Olive laughed. "Oh, we've plenty of land for our own needs, Farley. I just thought it was an interesting tidbit."

"Really? An interesting tidbit?"

In the back of her mind, Cassidy heard the percolating rumbles of the approaching thunderstorm. But she had nothing to fear from thunder and lightning. It was her mother who had her all riled up.

And she just couldn't take it anymore.

"Go on, Mom, why don't you connect all the dots for Farley? In case he's so stupid he can't see that if he and I marry it will be so wonderful that our land is connected."

"Whoa, Cass. You're getting a little crazy here," Corb said.

"Am I? It isn't just Mother behind this. You think I didn't notice the way all of you herded Farley and me into these two back seats—like we were cattle going up the ramp to the loading chute."

"Cassidy!" Olive threw down her napkin.

An eerie silence fell over the table. It was as though the entire ranch was holding its breath.

Then, in the next second, came a crash of thunder

that had the dishes dancing on the table. Cassidy was already standing by then.

"I think it would be a good idea if I went to the barn and checked on the horses."

No one said a word to her as she left the room.

FARLEY WANTED TO laugh. Or maybe cheer. But he didn't think either reaction would sit well with the Lamberts. And though they were friends, Coffee Creek Ranch was also his biggest client.

So he held his tongue and just listened as Olive apologized for the rudeness of her daughter.

"I didn't think she was all that rude," he said calmly. "You gotta admit she was provoked." He glanced around the table. Olive had an expression of wide-eyed innocence, but no one else would meet his gaze. "You all were a little obvious," he added.

"I don't know what you're talking about, Dan Farley." Olive started gathering plates, even though most of them hadn't finished eating. "Cassidy thinks everything is all about her. It never occurred to her that maybe Laurel wanted to sit by Corb and that's why— Oh, bother. It's just too silly to put into words."

Olive was doing a good job of obfuscating, but Corb, Laurel and Jackson were smirking. They knew a con job when they heard one.

"Guilty as charged," said Corb, shaking his head. "Sorry, buddy. Seems real stupid now, but we did kind of arrange things so you two sat together."

"Corb!"

"Cassidy does take a lot of wisecracks from her brothers," Laurel said diplomatically.

"Come on, honey. We're just having fun. It's no big deal."

"Well, it is to your sister," Farley pointed out. "She feels like she's being railroaded." And not for the first time, he guessed. It couldn't be easy being the youngest, and the only girl, in a family as strong-willed as this one.

They didn't mean to run roughshod over her. But what none of them seemed to understand was that beneath her tough, spunky attitude, she was soft and vulnerable.

A side she tended to only reveal when she was around the animals she loved. Sky, Lucy…Finnegan.

He understood better now why she was so determined to start a new life for herself in Billings.

Chapter Eleven

On Monday the phone rang while Cassidy was having breakfast with her mother. Olive was preparing to give a tour to some buyers who were driving up from Bozeman in about an hour, while Cassidy was waiting for Farley to come by and grab a mucus sample from Finn.

Her mustang had showed a bit more appetite again this morning, and Cassidy was really hopeful that the test would be clear of the strangles bacteria.

Her mother wasn't talking to her much today. She was still wounded by the scene Cassidy had made at last night's dinner.

Cassidy figured she should be the one who was wounded. But as time went by she felt more and more guilty. She hated discord and her mother's silent treatment was the worst.

"It's for you."

Those were the first words her mother had said to her all morning. "Thanks, Mom." Cassidy took the receiver, resisting the urge to move to another room.

"Hello, this is Cassidy Lambert."

"Nice to speak to you, Ms. Lambert. This is Pamela Oswald from Cushman and Green."

Cassidy froze. Finally they were getting back to her. But she'd checked on Facebook last night and several more of her classmates had reported being given second interviews last week.

So maybe now they were calling the rejects?

She tried to prepare herself for disappointment. She didn't want to fall apart. Not in front of her mother.

"I've been looking forward to hearing from you, too," she replied.

"I'm glad. Because we were hoping you would come to our offices for a second interview. We'd like you to meet a few more people in our organization and give them a chance to get to know you, as well."

Cassidy pumped her arm. Yes! "That would be great." Was that too colloquial? "I mean, I'd be happy to come to Billings."

"Would Thursday suit you? Say at nine?"

"That sounds perfect."

"Great. Just go to the main reception desk and ask for me. I'll send you an email confirming the details, in case you don't have a pen and paper handy right now."

"Thanks so much, Ms. Cushman. I mean Oswald." Cassidy's insides cringed at the mistake, but the woman on the phone didn't even seem to notice as she thanked her again, then said goodbye.

Cassidy replaced the phone. Her mother had been watching her, but now she seemed busy stacking the dishwasher. When she was done, she washed her hands, then finally looked at her daughter.

"I suppose that was the accounting firm you've been waiting to hear from?"

Heck and darn. She wanted to be happy about this. Instead, she felt almost guilty. "They've invited me for a second interview on Thursday."

"So soon?"

Three days' notice didn't seem unreasonable to Cassidy, but she nodded.

"Well, I guess we'll all just chip in and work a little harder around here."

There were actual tears in Olive's eyes as she said this. Tears that Cassidy knew would have any one of her brothers jumping hoops to try to clear away.

But Cassidy knew there was no way to do that. She'd told her mom that she wasn't going to be a regular part of the team that ran Coffee Creek Ranch. No matter how many times she said it, her mother never seemed to hear.

Her mother *didn't want* to hear. Maybe a good daughter would behave different. Cassidy knew she couldn't.

She *would* go on that interview.

And, if she was offered the job, she *would* take it.

MONDAY MORNING FARLEY took a few hours at his desk to catch up on paperwork and follow through with test results. He was pleased to see that the cultures for both Lucy and Chickweed from Coffee Creek Ranch were negative for S. equi.

Finnegan's, however, was still positive. But this was the sample he'd taken last week. He'd get another today and hopefully that one would reveal better news.

He pulled up his sheet with the calls he needed to make today. Liz always prepared this for him, right after she made their morning coffee.

Looked like he had another long day to put in, but that was springtime in ranch country for you. Frankly, Coffee Creek Ranch was getting big enough that they could almost use a full-time vet. Monahan's equine center—a horse training and boarding facility on the other side of town—was his other major client. They employed a full-time farrier, but he was often called out to help there, as well.

And he was still trying to service the other thirty or so ranchers in the area. Thankfully, most of them were a hell of a lot smaller, many more like acreages than real farms or ranches.

Still they all had animals. And most anyone who had domesticated animals, whether cows, horses, dogs, cats, or even—as in the case of the Bernhard family— lizards, eventually needed a vet.

"So."

He heard Liz enter his office and plant herself in the vacant chair.

When she didn't say anything further, he looked up from his papers. Normally Liz was a pretty upbeat person. Today she didn't seem that happy. "Yes, Liz?"

"I have a friend whose son just graduated from vet school in Washington. He met a girl from Lewiston while he was there. She also graduated from vet school, by the way. They're planning on getting married and moving to the area. You could either sit back and let them become your competition. Or you could hire them and train them so they actually learn to become decent veterinarians."

"It's not enough that you arrange my dates. Now you're hiring the staff, too?"

"Look, it's a lead, okay? Would it hurt to interview them?" She set two résumés on his desk. "Don't know why I bother. I give you the best advice in the world and you never follow it."

He sighed. "I take it you spoke to Amber this weekend?"

"You mean the prettiest, nicest and most eligible woman in the county? Yes, I did."

Prettiest? No.

Nicest? Maybe. If by *nice* you meant bland.

And he could name one other woman who was just as eligible as Amber Ellis. Not that it made any difference to him. He was pretty sure after Sunday dinner he'd made it to Cassidy's "no fly" list.

"Liz, you know chemistry is a big *X* factor. You can take a man and a woman that you think would make a perfect couple and it just doesn't work out that way."

"Yeah. Maybe that was the problem. Or maybe Cassidy Lambert came back to town and—"

"Liz." He used her name like a big, forceful stop sign. "Off-limits, Liz."

She looked startled. And well she might. He'd never said that to her before.

But no way, no how, was he discussing Cassidy with her.

Silently, she gave him a resentful look, then left the room. He waited until she'd closed the door before he checked his list again.

How about that? First stop: Coffee Creek Ranch.

FARLEY DROVE UP to the Lamberts' home barn about fifteen minutes later. Today he was just making a quick trip, to get a sample from Finnegan, then he was off to the other side of the county for a long day of preg-testing on the Double D.

He slipped on his stethoscope and a pair of gloves before stepping into the quarantine area. He found Cassidy giving her mustang a gentle rubdown.

Lucky horse.

She was in those jeans she always wore. He'd noticed the label when he'd washed them. Tuff, they were called.

Sexy, was what he called them. They made her legs look long and slender and her rear end unbelievably cute.

She had on an old T-shirt today, only partially tucked in, but he didn't mind that. Cassidy was at her best when she looked disheveled.

"Hey, Farley." She kept brushing her horse, but he could see a flush working its way up her neck to her fair cheeks. "I'm sorry about last night. I hope I didn't embarrass you too much."

"It'd take a lot more than that to get me embarrassed. I thought it was kind of funny to tell you the truth." He went on the other side of Finnegan, listened to his heart and lungs and frowned. Not what he'd been hoping for. "How's our boy doing today?"

"He ate a little. Not as much as I'd like." Cassidy paused. "I wish I could find those scenes with my mother funny. I try to let it all slide off me, the way Corb does. But she gets to me. She really does."

"They say mother-daughter relationships can be tricky. Not that I know firsthand." He pulled a swab kit out of his case and quickly took another sample.

Then he checked Finn's temperature, frowning again when he saw it was thirty-nine degrees. He said nothing to Cassidy, though, not wanting to worry her.

"I'll get back to you on the test. But I have a feeling it may be a while before we get this bug completely out of his system. In the meantime, you can let Lucy and Chickweed rejoin the herd. Their tests came out negative again."

"They'll be so glad about that. And so will I. They've been so frisky lately I can't seem to give them enough exercise."

"Been barrel racing with Lucy again?" He hoped so. He'd loved watching Cassidy on the palomino. The golden girl and her golden horse. Even more appealing than the picture they'd made, however, had been the way they worked together as a unit.

"Maybe I will this afternoon." Cassidy put down the curry brush, then hitched her thumbs in her belt loops and followed him out of the stall. "It's fun for both of us, though I suspect Mom and Corb would prefer I got some more work done."

"Exercising horses is work," Farley insisted. "I still think you should give some thought to registering at Rogue River."

Cassidy laughed. "And give my mother something else to complain about? Believe me, one rodeo cowboy is enough for this family. Besides, if things go my way on Thursday, I won't have much opportunity for that sort of thing anymore."

Her eyes were sparkling, as if she was sitting on some sort of secret. Though he had a sense he wasn't going to like it, he asked anyway.

"What's happening Thursday?"

"I got a call for a second interview with Cushman and Green!"

He forced a smile. "Congratulations. That's the accounting firm, right?"

With her hands pressed together under her chin, she nodded. "Most of my friends had already heard from them. I'd lost all hope that I would be chosen. And then this morning, they phoned."

Farley felt as if a big, black storm cloud had just pushed the sunshine out of the day. But he smiled again and told her she should be proud.

"Thank you. The timing couldn't be better. After that scene with my mother…" Cassidy kicked at a clump of hay, scattering the fibers over the floor. "I truly believe we'll have a better relationship if we don't see so much of each other."

"So what are you thinking? Coming home maybe once a year?" Farley tried to joke so she wouldn't guess how he really felt.

She laughed. "More like once a month. I will miss this place. But I was thinking if I found a ground-level suite maybe I could take Sky with me this time."

"It won't be easy for her to adjust to the city." Farley waved a hand indicating all the beautiful land around them. "Not when she's used to all this."

Once more the smile on Cassidy's face wavered, but then she shrugged. "We'll see. She's getting older. Maybe she won't mind spending most of her days inside."

Farley removed the protective gloves, then washed up at the sink. He thought he could sense some nervousness behind her happy chatter.

But that was only normal, right? It didn't mean she had doubts that she was doing the right thing.

Whereas he did. He couldn't help siding with her family on this one. Cassidy belonged here, in Coffee Creek. But if he dared to tell her this, he'd only be one more person telling her how to live.

CASSIDY DROVE TO Billings on Wednesday after her evening chores. Finnegan hadn't been cleared from quarantine yet—and frankly he didn't seem quite himself, anyway—so she asked Corb if he would keep an eye on him for her.

Her brother must have been feeling a little guilty about Sunday, because he didn't tease her or complain, just said it would be no problem.

Even though she knew it was. His days were full

with branding and vaccinating the new calves, but she didn't want to ask one of the hired hands to do the job.

Not that she didn't trust them. She just trusted Corb more.

The drive to Billings was long. Three hours. She'd expected to enjoy the journey, but thoughts of home—and Farley—kept intruding.

He'd seemed happy for her when she told him about the second interview. She'd been glad of the support—which she hadn't received from her family.

But part of her had wished he would just grab her and kiss her.

Ever since that night at his house, she'd been able to think of little else but making love with Farley. What would it be like? Would it ever happen?

So much was against them. Their age difference had been a big impediment for a long time. And now there was her mother—pushing them together so hard that Cassidy couldn't help but wonder if she was in danger of making a big mistake.

If she succumbed to her longing for Farley, she'd be trapped. Just the way her mother wanted her to be. Living forever in the shadow of her family and the Coffee Creek Ranch.

Cassidy spent a lonely night at the Super 8. She could have called her classmates—and Josh—but she didn't want to talk to any of them until she had the interview behind her.

If it was a flop, she'd just run back home and consider her options.

If it went well, she'd be in the mood for a little celebrating.

Thursday morning she dressed in the same skirt, blazer, blouse and pumps that she'd worn to the first interview when the firms had come on campus to survey the best of that year's graduating class.

She hoped they wouldn't remember that she was wearing the same outfit. But she had nothing else appropriate.

She winced as she walked out of the hotel to the parking lot. She wished she'd had the nerve to wear her cream-colored cowboy boots. But her girlfriends in college had told her the look wasn't right.

She sighed and slid behind the driver's wheel. She'd gone over the directions on the internet so many times, she had no need to refer to a map as she made her way toward the downtown.

Billings was small as cities went, with around a quarter of a million people. But it was the biggest metropolis in Montana and as she surveyed the busy streets, the traffic and all the people hurrying to work, she wondered if she was going to be happy here.

She'd been fine during her five years in Bozeman. But that had been college. This could be the rest of her life—at least a big chunk of it.

In her email Pamela Oswald had helpfully suggested a place to park and Cassidy felt more confident once she'd maneuvered her truck into one of the stalls. On foot she felt better. Well, if it wasn't for these darn heels, she'd feel better. Why had she let the girls talk her into three-inch heels?

She hoped she didn't look as if she'd been hobbled as she made her way along the sidewalk toward North Broadway and what appeared to be the tallest office tower in the city. Around her men and women were carrying briefcases and take-out coffees. Many of them had PDAs in hand, checking messages or taking calls.

She felt important, just being among them.

Squaring her shoulders, she entered the lobby and headed for the elevators, squishing into the small space with four men and three other ladies.

She noticed a few glances coming her way, and nervously put a hand to her hair.

On Tuesday she'd gone to Lewistown to get it trimmed. "Chop off three or four inches" had been her instructions. When she looked at the floor, though, she was sure she saw at least six inches of her golden hair—gone.

The new length came to her shoulders, though, and swung nicely as she walked. This morning she'd used a hair dryer and straightener after her shower to make sure it was sleek and controlled.

Stop thinking about your hair, stupid. It's your brain that will win you this job.

She got off on the fifteenth floor and headed to the receptionist, per Pamela's instructions.

She was invited to wait on an elegant leather sofa. Business publications and the *Wall Street Journal* were fanned out on the glass table in front of her. But she focused on all the people coming and going. Some of them cast her a curious look. A few smiled. Most just ignored her.

If her spine had been replaced with an iron rod, she couldn't have sat any straighter. Everything felt so foreign. The people weren't just dressed differently, they spoke differently and moved differently.

Finally Pamela came and she was so polished and elegant that Cassidy felt like a complete country bumpkin. She'd never thought to get gel nails. Or to wear jewelry. Not that she owned anything as chic as the chunky silver necklace and bracelet that looked so great with Pamela's black suit.

Those little touches make all the difference, she thought. And then she reminded herself, *It's about your brain. Okay?*

She was given a tour of the offices. Hallways lined with oil paintings, board rooms with sleek furniture and views that spread out to the Beartooth Mountains.

She was introduced to people she'd never remember. There was a little banter and quite a few smiles, but mostly people were very serious.

Fifteen minutes later, she was in an accounting partner's office. He looked about Farley's age, but was as different as could be from the country veterinarian. Thin brown hair, trendy glasses, an expensive suit that fit his slender build as if it had been sewn in place.

"It's nice to meet you, Cassidy," said Mr. Cushman—not *the* Cushman for whom the business had been named, but a nephew, Pamela had explained in a whisper a few minutes earlier.

"Thank you. I'm happy to be here, too."

He shuffled papers on his desk. "With the downturn in the economy we only have room for three articling students this year. If I was going on marks alone, you'd be a shoo-in."

Cassidy swallowed nervously, then managed a slight smile.

"But we have to see how you'll fit in here. That's why we asked you to come and look around, meet a few people."

They chatted for about ten minutes. Cassidy thought he seemed impressed that she knew the names of the firm's biggest clients and was up-to-date on local business news.

This was all research she'd done a month ago before the first interview.

Then he invited her to lunch. They were joined by a couple of articling students who'd been hired last year, and went to eat at a posh restaurant with names of things on the menu that she didn't recognize and waiters so attentive they folded her napkin on her chair when she went to the restroom.

At the conclusion of the meal she and Pamela had a final chat. "It was a pleasure meeting you, Cassidy. The partners will be making their final decision in a couple of weeks and I'll phone you as soon as I know."

Chapter Twelve

Cassidy decided to spend the night in Billings, rather than drive home right away. The day had taken a lot of energy out of her. She wandered the streets, finding a charming area with shops and restaurants. She picked up a slice of pizza from a take-out place and found a bench where she could relax and people-watch.

She didn't need to be alone. She could have called Josh or one of her other friends. But she was too worried that if they started comparing notes about their interviews, she would discover hers hadn't gone as well as she thought it had.

Around eight o'clock she went back to the motel room, watched some TV, then went to sleep. She was up early the next day, on the road by seven, and home just before ten.

Her mother happened to be locking the front door when Cassidy pulled up to her parking spot. But as usual, her warmest welcome came from her dog. Sky was as amazed and delighted to see her as if she'd been gone for a month.

Cassidy was pleased to see her wound was healing nicely and her eyes were bright and lively.

After giving Sky one last scratch, she straightened. "Hi, Mom."

Olive was dressed in working clothes—jeans, shirt, old boots and a bandana at her neck. This could mean only one thing. Corb had organized a big work party to push the cattle farther north.

"How was the interview?"

"I'm not sure. I have to wait a few weeks now for them to decide." She gave her mother a kiss on the cheek, then tugged her bandana lightly. "I take it you're going with the guys to move cattle?"

Olive nodded. "We'll be camping out tonight, home around dinnertime tomorrow." She hesitated. "Want to come along? Dave is staying back to keep an eye on the animals. He knows to feed Sky. And check in on Finn."

Dave was one of the extra hands B.J. had hired after Brock's death. And he'd turned out to be a reliable worker, from what Corb and Jackson said. But Cassidy didn't want to leave the care of her animals to someone who wasn't family.

Normally staying back from a trip like this would have been a major sacrifice. Without a doubt, Cassidy's happiest childhood memories were the family trail rides when they'd moved the cattle up to higher elevations where the grass was just coming in nice and thick. The days were long but there was always time to enjoy the scenery, be amused by the cattle's antics, and indulge in late-night conversations around a campfire.

But that wasn't for her. Not this year, anyway.

"No. I'm tired. And I have things to do."

"Things like what?" Her mother sounded cautious.

"Just things, Mom. You go and have fun. I'll take care of business around here."

CASSIDY QUICKLY CHANGED into regular work clothes, then went to the home barn to see everyone off on the trail ride. There were bedrolls behind the saddles and a couple of extra horses carried the tents and food supplies. She felt another pang of regret. Nothing tasted better than a meal cooked over a campfire.

"Sure you don't want to join us?" Corb asked. "We can wait while you saddle up."

"That's okay." She looked over the crew. Besides her mother and Corb, there was also Jackson and three hired wranglers. "What are Laurel and the baby doing while you're away?"

"She's gone to Highwood to visit Winnie and the baby. Eugenia, Vince and Dawn are holding down the fort at the café while she's gone."

Five minutes later they were off and Cassidy headed for the open barn door. She passed Dave Crosby at the boot dip, on his way out.

A smile broke on his weathered thirtyish face. "Hey, you're back. That's good. I was just heading over to check the new calves and moms in the cattle barn, but I'm kind of worried about that mustang of yours."

"Finnegan? What's the problem?"

"Well, shortly after you left on Wednesday he went off his food."

"I thought Corb was looking after him?"

"Yeah, well, your brother asked me to look in on him. And I noticed yesterday morning he hadn't touched his oats. Not today, either."

"But I wasn't feeding him oats. There was this special formula. I left the instructions on a sheet in the feed room."

Dave scratched behind his ear. "Well, I didn't see those. And no one told me any different. So I fed him oats, same as we usually do."

"Okay, Dave." She put a hand on his arm, then nodded for him to go. "I'll handle it from here."

She wasn't going to blame him, and not Corb, either. She shouldn't have left Finnegan. It was as simple as that.

She hurried inside and was not happy at what she saw. Finnegan was visibly thinner and weaker. "Hey, boy, what's the problem?" She patted him down carefully. His belly had swollen, but she couldn't find any of the pustules around his neck or throat the way she had with Lucy and Chickweed.

Obviously, she had been wrong to assume he was out of the woods.

She went to mix up the gruel that she'd fed him with success before, but today he would have none of it. Not even a bite.

"Oh, Finn. You need to eat. I can see how weak you are."

Finn just snorted and looked at her with the saddest set of horse eyes she'd ever seen.

She moved Finn to a fresh stall, offered him water and feed again, but he still refused to eat. Feeling desperate, she called Farley's cell phone number. He didn't answer and the call was routed through to his office.

"Farley & Sons," said Liz Moffat.

"Hey, Liz, this is Cassidy out at Coffee Creek. My mustang has taken a turn for the worse." She'd been so sure he was getting better. There was no way she would have left him if she'd thought he might have a setback. "He hasn't eaten in a few days and he seems awfully weak. Do you think this is a complication from the strangles?"

"I couldn't say. But I do know that last test came up positive, so he still has the bacteria." Liz's voice had been cool at first, but now she sounded genuinely concerned. "Unfortunately Farley's on the Double D again today, working out in the fields where cell phone reception can be spotty."

"Oh, heck and darn…"

"Isn't it always the way?" Liz agreed. "But if I can be sure of anything, it's this. Once Farley gets your message, he's going to be there to help you as soon as humanly possible. Maybe even five minutes faster than that."

CASSIDY TURNED ON the radio to keep them company, set out a water dish for Sky and made herself a pot of coffee. There wasn't much she could do for Finnegan, but give him a lot of TLC.

And wait for Farley. He'd know what to do when he got there. They just had to be patient.

But the sun was skimming the tops of the western ranges by the time she heard his truck pulling up to the barn.

Dave had left for home two hours ago. He'd asked if he could do anything to help before he headed off but she'd said not to worry.

"The vet will be here soon."

She had the door to the barn open, hoping the fresh air might help Finnegan. The horse was lying down in his stall now—and had been for about three hours. She watched as Farley climbed out of his truck. He looked tired as he lugged his vet bag out of the passenger seat and he held his head kind of low, so she couldn't see his eyes from beneath the rim of his hat until he was almost beside her.

And when their gazes finally did connect, she saw

the same cool, dispassionate look he'd had a month ago when they'd happened into the café at the same time.

Farley didn't say hello or ask about her trip. He looked from her, to her horse, then turned on one of the lights and moved into the stall. "How long since he's eaten?"

"It sounds like he hasn't had anything since I left for Billings on Wednesday." She squeezed her hands nervously together as she waited for Farley to do his thing.

He had his stethoscope around his neck and a rectal thermometer in his hand. After fifteen minutes, he heaved a heavy sigh. "Well, he's still running that fever. And I don't like the sound of his heart. See the way he's sticking his legs out?"

She nodded. She'd never noticed Finn rest in that position before.

"That tells me he's in pain. My guess is that the strangles bacteria has progressed to his vital organs." Farley ran a hand over Finnegan's stomach. "See that swelling? It probably hurts him to eat."

"Poor Finn." She knelt on the soft bedding and wrapped her arms around Finnegan's neck. The horse gave no reaction, but close like this, she could hear the labored sound of his breathing. "So what do we do?"

Farley didn't answer.

The truth crept in slowly with the inevitability of the sun setting behind the mountains. And with it came a pain and a sorrow that Cassidy already had too much familiarity with.

She'd been fifteen when her father died.

Twenty-four when Brock was killed in the accident.

And now it was Finnegan's turn.

Just a horse, some might say. But he'd been family. And one of the last links she still had to her dad.

Farley sat down a few feet from her, leaning his back against the side wall of the stall. He watched Finnegan for a while, then he looked at her.

Cassidy didn't want to see the sympathy in his eyes. She bent her head close to Finn's and murmured words that she hoped were comforting. "Don't be scared, Finn. I'm not leaving you again."

Her voice broke a little on the last word. Would this have happened if she hadn't gone to Billings?

And, as if he had read her mind, Farley said, "There's not much you can do to prevent this kind of complication. Finnegan is an old horse. That made him more susceptible."

"H-he's very near the end, isn't he?"

Farley nodded.

Her eyes started filling with tears. But she smiled. "I remember the day Finn came to us. The whole family had gone to a horse sale. It was my eighth birthday. We didn't have the breeding business back then, Mom and Dad were just looking for good cattle horses. I was the one who spotted Finnegan first."

The memory was fresh and true. She could almost smell the stockyard, taste the popcorn—each of them had been given a small bag—and hear the rapid-fire sound of the auctioneer's voice.

"'Look at that one,' I told my dad. 'Your sister has a good eye,' he said." Cassidy smiled, remembering the approving look her dad had given her.

"My brothers all crowded in to see him, but Finnegan would have nothing to do with them. He walked right up to me, though. And Dad said, 'Look at that. I guess we'll have to buy our girl a horse for her birthday.'

"Mom was appalled. She thought he was too much horse for an eight-year-old to handle. And of course she was right. But Dad told me that if I took care of him for two years, by the time I was ten I'd be able to ride him. I remember sitting on the fence watching as Dad trained him. Dad had such a calm and patient way with horses. I learned a lot just observing him. At the end of each session, it was my job to clean the tack and give Finnegan a good brushing. And while I was working the curry comb I'd be dreaming of the day when I'd finally be able to ride him…"

"And ride him you did." Farley had one hand on Finnegan's back, as if reassuring the horse that he, too, wasn't going anywhere. "I used to think that you were mighty small to be on such a big horse. But right from the start, you knew how to control him. The two of you made quite the pair."

Cassidy swallowed. Those had been such happy days. The strengths and weaknesses of her mother and father had been complementary. Between them, they'd created a family that was strong and loyal with love as a solid core.

The balance had been lost, however, when her dad died.

"When we got home from the hospital after Dad passed away, I headed straight to the barn and took Finnegan out for a ride. I was a mess, but Finnegan seemed to know that he had to be good and gentle with me that day. We were out for hours, and you know something strange?"

Farley didn't say anything, but his eyes told her he was listening with both his ears and his heart.

"I felt as if my dad was with us. I talked to him and I swear he answered me…" She brushed the tears from her eyes and tried to smile. "Crazy, huh?"

"No. It just shows the bond you had with your father."

Cassidy let out a long breath and looked down at Finnegan. Her heart ached to see him so still and weak. "Are you suffering, Finn? I'm so sorry if you are. You were such a good horse. So brave and true. I won't forget you. Not ever."

She laid her head close to his and Finnegan gave a soft nicker. It was the last sound she heard him make. The barn suddenly felt incredibly silent and cold.

"He's gone. Isn't he?"

"Yes. I'm sorry. But yes."

"No." She didn't want it to be true. She wrapped her arms tighter around her horse and though she'd wanted to be strong, she couldn't help herself. The sobs came pouring out of her, as if she'd had a broken heart for years and was only now letting it all out.

She was crying for Finn. And Brock. And her father.

Crying for a time when they'd all been together. Those glorious years that she'd taken for granted, never guessing how soon they would end.

"Come here, sweetheart." Farley had laid a blanket over Finn. Now he pulled her up and into his arms, not seeming to mind that her face was wet and sticky. He put a hand on her head, letting her burrow into the solid warmth of his chest.

And she clung for a good long minute, then took a deep breath.

"I'm sorry I lost it."

"I wouldn't think much of you if you hadn't."

There were tears in his eyes, too, she saw. She reached up to touch one. Farley caught her hand and held it close.

"Now what?" she asked, her voice coming out in tremolo.

"I know you have a plot where you bury your horses.

Let me make the arrangements for that tomorrow. When your family gets home you can have a ceremony."

"Thank you."

"In the meantime, you and Sky should come home with me. You shouldn't be alone tonight."

Hearing her name, Sky came immediately to Cassidy's side. She'd been standing guard at the door all this time, Cassidy realized, as if sensing they needed protection.

"Good girl, Sky." She petted her dog and considered Farley's offer.

Her instinct was to say no. But she knew if she spent the night in her mother's house, or even in Brock's cabin, all she would think about was Finnegan growing cold and stiff in the barn. She shuddered.

Farley took her hand. "Let's get your things."

It was too hot for a fire this evening. Farley went around his house opening windows, but the air still felt humid and close. He made soup and tomato sandwiches, and though Cassidy swore she wasn't hungry, he noticed she ate every bite.

When they were done, they took a couple beers and went out on the porch. Sky, seeing what they were doing, turned back at the door and returned to the hearth with the other dogs.

Not wanting to attract the moths, Farley didn't light the candles that he kept out here. There was enough light filtering out from the living room window that they could see where they were going. They sat side by side on the cushioned swing and listened to the cricket music.

"So how was the trip to Billings?" he finally asked.

He'd been avoiding the subject, not sure he was ready to hear the answer.

He'd had a rough couple days while she was gone. It had taken her absence from Coffee Creek to make him realize how far gone he was.

He ought to be protecting himself from more pain and keeping his distance. But seeing her in pain made it impossible for him to stay away.

"It was fine, I hope. They seemed impressed with my academic record. And my meetings went well." Cassidy took a swallow of beer, then pushed out of the swing and went to stand by the railing.

She looked gorgeous. Her hair was shorter, but it suited her and it was still long enough to frame her beautiful face in gold. Before coming here she'd changed into clean jeans and a T-shirt and he couldn't help noticing that her silver belt buckle fell at just the right spot to emphasize both her slender waist and the curve of her hips.

He felt his heart start to pound, hard and fast.

She always did this to him. Always.

He found the courage to ask, "Did you get the job?"

She sighed. "I don't know yet."

But she would, he thought. Who wouldn't hire a smart, beautiful woman like her? Who could resist?

The realization that she was really going scooped all the feeling from his gut, leaving him hollow and exposed. And angry. Why did he care so much? He shouldn't. He'd known from the start what her plans were and frankly, he couldn't really blame her. Being a Lambert wasn't easy for her. In Billings, she could finally just be herself.

"If I hadn't gone, maybe Finn would still be alive."

She took a long drink, emptying the can then setting it aside. She turned to stare out at the night.

"I don't think that's true."

"But you can't *know* it isn't." Her voice cracked and then she was crying again. "No one else loved him like I do. I should have known they wouldn't give him enough attention."

"No." He hated hearing her suffering. He went to her, putting his arms around her. "Don't blame yourself. Even if you'd been by his side every second, there was nothing you could have done."

She turned into him, pressing her face, damp with tears, against his chest. He cupped the back of her head with his hands, feeling all sorts of things that were complicated and wrong.

He wanted to comfort her and reassure her.

But he also wanted…

And then she was lifting her face and bringing her hands to his shoulders. "Farley?"

She said his name softly, almost as if she was pleading for something. And then she was on her toes. And he was leaning closer to her. And they were kissing.

Chapter Thirteen

Farley made it all disappear. Every worry, every loss, every problem. Gone.

Instead Cassidy had him and this moment. His bronzed skin and taut muscles, his amazing kisses and his pleasure-giving hands.

She stopped thinking.

There was no need to think. Their bodies were in control now. One kiss led to another. Clothing was discarded. They didn't go inside. She didn't want that. Farley grabbed the cushion from the swing and set her gently onto that.

She supposed she could have seen the stars and the moon as they made love. But Farley's eyes were enough. His eyes told her that he knew what she needed. And knew how to give it to her.

As she cried out his name, she felt as if she were howling at the moon. And when he gasped her name back to her, the circle was complete. The waves of pleasure slowly ebbed, until all she could hear was his heart under her ear, and all she felt was his body next to hers.

"No wonder I was so afraid of you at the Harvest Dance."

"Why do you say that? Did I hurt you?"

"The opposite of hurt, I'd say. But was I ready for

this four years ago? I'd have to say no." She wasn't so sure she'd been ready now. She'd lost herself for a while there. Been consumed by all the things he made her feel.

And while it had been wonderful, it was also terrifying.

She'd only just started figuring out who she was. She didn't want to lose herself to Farley next. And that would be all too easy to do.

"Cass?" He brushed her hair gently with his fingers, letting the strands fall slowly back in place. "I'm sorry I couldn't save your horse for you."

She swallowed as the pain, momentarily pushed aside, started to seep back. "You did what you could. And maybe it was his time."

She rolled over and searched for her clothing. He must be thinking she and her mother were quite the pair. Both of them throwing her at him in the most shameless way.

She pulled on her jeans and top, anxious to be covered. This had not been right. It wasn't the plan. "Farley, will you drive me home?"

He looked stricken. "I thought—"

"This was a mistake. I—I must have been crazy." It was a warm evening, but her teeth were chattering.

"Cass, please, stay the night. In the spare room if you want." Farley was up, pulling on his jeans, then wrapping his shirt around her shoulders. "You're shaking. Are you cold?"

She shook her head, passed him back his shirt. "I can't stay. I can't."

As he drove her home, Farley was reminded of that night, four years ago, when they'd sat silently in a dark truck, both of them desperate for the trip to be over so they could pretend the night had never happened.

Though Farley wasn't so sure he could make that same wish tonight. Making love with Cassidy had been everything and more that he could have hoped for. And she'd been right there with him. He'd heard the pleasure in her voice, felt it in her body, right down to her cells.

But emotionally she hadn't been ready. Maybe her emotions had been too raw. Maybe she saw him as a threat—someone else who would try to keep her from taking that job she wanted so much. Or maybe she just saw him as the man her mother wanted her to be with, and therefore the last man on earth she would ever settle for.

Just like on that other night, four years ago, when he stopped the truck, he went to open her door. Sky jumped out first, then Cassidy.

She wouldn't look him in the eyes. "Thanks for the lift, Farley. And thanks for…what you tried to do for Finn."

Every instinct screamed at him not to leave her this way. But what choice did he have?

"Let me walk you to the door."

She shook her head. "Just go, Farley, okay?"

She was so tired, she was swaying on her feet. Her face was tear-stained and her hand rested on Sky's head as if her dog was the only thing holding her together right now. He wanted to scoop her up and carry her to her bed.

Instead, he got back into the truck and drove away.

CASSIDY WATCHED UNTIL his taillights were faded to tiny dots in the distance, then contemplated her options. Sleep in the posh bedroom her mom had designed for her?

No, thanks.

She decided to drive to Brock's cabin and spend the night there. Sky was confused, but obeyed her command to climb into the passenger side of her truck. At the cabin, she found the key under the flowerpot as usual and went inside.

Sky seemed immediately at home and went to lie on the sofa. But Cassidy hung back. She hadn't been here since Brock's death and she felt as if she was violating a sacred space. As she moved tentatively from room to room, however, she began to feel a peaceful connection to her brother.

Cassidy looked over his music collection and found an album that he had played incessantly when he was around fourteen. She put it on and smiled at the familiar opening guitar riff.

The music filled up the empty spaces in the cabin and added warmth and life. Bonny had boxed Brock's belongings and given the cabin a cleaning after his death. Dust had accumulated over the passing months, but it wasn't too bad.

Cassidy found clean sheets in the linen cupboard and made up the spare bed. She turned on the shower, stripped and stepped inside. The hot water was soothing, at first. But it didn't take long for her thoughts to start torturing her. First she was sobbing, thinking of Finn.

And not a minute later, her breath was heavy, remembering what had happened with Farley. She ran a soapy cloth over her body. He'd touched her here. And here. And here.

Oh, Lord, what had possessed her? She'd practically begged him to make love to her, then treated him like chopped liver when it was over.

She'd been such a jerk. Just like four years ago. The parallel between the way she'd behaved on the two occasions was mortifying. How could she ever face him again?

Eventually the water began to run cool, and Cassidy switched off the taps. She dried off and then dragged her weary body to bed. Not a minute later, Sky joined her there.

Poor dog must be so confused by now. It had been quite an evening. First she'd been dragged out to the barn, then to Farley's place, and now here they were settling in at Brock's cabin.

Showing a wonderful ability to adapt to new circumstances, however, Sky just put down her head and went to sleep.

And Cassidy, eventually, did the same.

CASSIDY COULDN'T REMEMBER the last time she'd slept much past dawn. But she was exhausted—mentally and physically—and not only did the cabin's spare bedroom window face north, but the curtains were drawn. Finally, there was no alarm set in the room. In fact, there wasn't even a clock.

Sky must have been just as tired as she was, because she didn't wake Cassidy up, either.

It was the rumble of her empty stomach that finally roused Cassidy and had her lifting her head from the pillow.

She glanced around the dimly lit room in confusion, then winced as everything came back to her.

She grabbed her phone from the bedside table and could not believe what she saw.

She'd slept until noon?

Hastily, she scrambled out of the bed, then dressed

in the clothes from the previous night. It was hard not to remember Farley's fingers on the buttons of her shirt, or the way he'd looked at her when they'd—

No.

She let Sky out for her morning constitutional, then opened the passenger door of her truck and urged Sky to jump in.

For the first time that Cassidy could remember, Sky balked.

"We're not going far," she promised the border collie. "Just home."

The word *home* seemed to convince her and Sky finally took her place. As Cassidy motored back along the graveled road, she could hear the sound of heavy equipment coming from the direction of the horse burial grounds.

Farley was living up to his promise to take care of Finn, and Cassidy was thankful that she wouldn't have to face the body when she went into the barn this morning.

But Dave had already done the chores, she noticed, as she made the rounds of the cattle and equine barns ten minutes later. She went to the home barn last and the first thing she noticed was the missing boot bath.

Inside were more changes. The stall where Finnegan had died last night was empty and perfectly clean.

Only one person could have done all this. She found his note in the tack room.

"I've disinfected Finn's stall, feeding pail and water trough and burned the bedding. You can consider this official notice that the quarantine on Coffee Creek Ranch is ended."

Cassidy read the note several times, closing her eyes

and letting a few more tears fall. How could he be so kind and thoughtful when she'd behaved like such a—

Words failed her.

She wanted to call him and thank him, but she guessed he might not be too happy to hear from her right now. In fact, she wouldn't blame him if he never wanted to see her again.

Cassidy got some horse treats from the feed room then went outside to the pasture. Lucy spotted her right away and came trotting over.

"Good girl, Lucy." She broke off a piece of the baked horse treat and gave the palomino a hug. She wondered what Lucy and the rest of the herd had made of the previous night's events.

She was certain that they knew Finn had died. She could tell by the way they huddled closely together, even though the day was sunny and warm.

When she'd finished feeding Lucy the treat, she patted her on the rump, then headed back to her truck. It was past one in the afternoon now and she needed coffee.

The Cinnamon Stick seemed like the logical place to go.

STRAWS MONAHAN WAS sitting in one of the booths, enjoying coffee and a sandwich. The gray-haired rancher was in his early fifties, a trim, kindly eyed man whose family roots in this area went back as far as the Lamberts and the Turners.

"Thanks," Cassidy said to Dawn, who was manning the café with Vince this afternoon. She picked up her coffee and sandwich. "How's it going? Has it been busy?"

"Steady, but not too bad. I hope Laurel manages to

talk Winnie into coming back to Coffee Creek soon.
I don't mind working the extra hours, but I miss Winnie. We all do."

"Yes, that would be good," Cassidy agreed. She
hoped her mother's note would be the first step in making Winnie want to come back to the town that she had
once called home.

Cassidy nodded hello to Straws, who'd been looking
her way ever since she'd stepped into the café. She was
heading outside, intending to sit on the bench in the sun
to eat her meal, when he called her over.

"Cassidy? Got a minute?"

"Sure." She settled herself into the bench seat opposite his. Back when the Monahans had been cattle
ranchers, Straws had been a successful rodeo cowboy,
as well. He'd retired when his wife had their first child,
about twenty-five years ago, and opened the Monahan
Rodeo Arena and Equestrian Center.

Over the years he'd built amazing facilities, including an eighty-thousand-square-foot indoor arena and
an outdoor stadium with seating for twenty thousand
people. These were used for all sorts of rodeo, riding
and equestrian clinics.

Cassidy had a lot of time for Straws, who was widely
known for his humane methods of training and working
with horses. He was scrupulous in the people he hired
and the Monahans' full-service boarding was generally
considered the best that money could buy for your horse.

"Has your mother talked you into joining our committee yet?" he asked.

It took her a moment to connect the dots. Then she
laughed. She'd forgotten that Straws was on her mom's
Heritage Site Committee. "No, but she hasn't given up
trying."

"Olive never does," Straws said mildly.

Cassidy wondered if he was going to try to persuade her as well, but his next question took a different tack.

"You were a barrel racer in high school, weren't you?"

"That was a while ago. But yes."

"You were very talented. I remember watching you when my own daughter was doing some competing. Ever consider going back to it?"

"Why do you ask?"

"I just lost one of my best riding and barrel racing instructors. She's marrying a fellow from New Mexico, leaving in about a week. Any chance you want the job?"

"Well—I'm flattered." And she was. Straws only hired the best. "But I just graduated from college and I'm planning to move to Billings and work for an accounting firm."

"Really? Olive never said anything about that."

Cassidy rolled her eyes. "She isn't exactly a fan of my plan."

He laughed. "She is skilled at ignoring facts that aren't to her suiting, isn't she? Well, if your plans change in the next few weeks, you let me know, okay? Even a few weeks of your time would tide me over until I found someone permanent."

"Thanks, Straws, I'll give it some thought."

Straws rose to leave, then hesitated as he noticed someone else come into the café.

Cassidy followed his gaze and was horrified to see Dan Farley at the entrance. He noticed her, too, but she couldn't decipher the look in his dark eyes.

"Hey, Farley. Come and join us." Oblivious to the emotional undercurrents flowing between Cassidy and Farley, Straws made room for Farley to sit next to him.

"I was just about to ask Cassidy here how their horses were making out. I heard you had some strangles to contend with?"

Cassidy noticed how tired Farley looked. She hated that it was her fault. She wrapped her hands around her mug of coffee then turned to Straws. "Quarantine was just lifted today. Two of our horses recovered, but…" She steeled herself to say the rest. "We did lose one of our older horses."

"I'm sorry to hear that. I hope it wasn't that beautiful palomino who died?"

"No. You've seen Lucky Lucy?"

He nodded. "I thought your mother was being a little foolhardy when she took her to Joe Purdy's ranch on the other side of Lewistown. Sure, Joe knows what he's doing when it comes to training barrel horses. But Purdy's has been battling with the infection for over a year. Never properly isolated and contained the disease when it first showed up and now it's spread pretty much through their entire herd."

Cassidy could see that Farley was as shocked to hear this as she was.

"I hadn't heard about that," Farley said slowly. "Purdy's ranch is well out of my district."

"When did Mom take Lucy to Joe Purdy's ranch?"

Straws wrinkled his brow. "Must have been mid-April."

Two weeks before Cassidy had come home from college. "Maybe she didn't know about the strangles?"

Straws shook his head. "I warned her myself."

A snippet of conversation came back to her then. "Farley, remember when you asked if any of our horses had left the property recently?"

He nodded, but didn't say anything. She knew he

was recalling how Jackson had mentioned seeing Olive load Lucky Lucy into a trailer and she'd insisted he was mistaken.

But this seemed to imply that Jackson had been telling the truth.

It was her mother who had lied. But why?

"Anyway, I'm glad it all worked out in the end." Straws finished his coffee. "I should hit the road. Cassidy, you think about my offer, you hear?" He winked. "I pay real good, in case you haven't heard."

Once the older rancher was gone, Farley lifted his brows. "Straws tried to hire you?"

"He's looking for a new riding teacher. Someone who knows how to barrel race." But who cared about such details now? "Farley, can you believe Mom would have exposed Lucy to strangles on purpose? It doesn't make sense. Everyone around knows that Straws has the best trainers in the area. And his operation is impeccable. If she wanted extra training for Lucy, why not take her to the Monahans'?"

"It doesn't make sense," he agreed.

Unless… "You don't think she did it on purpose because of me? I hate to sound paranoid, but she might have figured that if a couple of our horses came down with strangles, I'd be home in a few weeks and I'd be the obvious person to look after them."

"That's twisted. But there is a certain logic to it," Farley said.

Plus, Cassidy thought, not only had the strangles kept her on the ranch, it had forced her into spending time with Dan Farley—the man Olive thought she should marry.

But that part was just too embarrassing to say out loud.

"This is crazy, isn't it? Mom can be manipulative,

but she'd never go this far. She's too good of a business person to risk spreading strangles over her entire herd."

Farley was quiet for a while. Then in a low voice he said, "Maybe she took a calculated risk. She knew the riding horses were separated from the breeding ones, and the chances of the quarter horses getting infected were slim. Plus, she probably knows that only ten percent of the horses who develop strangles ever develop complications. Maybe she hoped your horses would ride it out without any lasting problems."

"Or maybe she'd calculated all that and concluded that the loss of a horse or two would be worth it," Cassidy concluded bitterly.

Farley rubbed his forehead then sighed. "You know what? I think the drama of the past few days is catching up to us. There's a much more likely scenario."

"Really? I'd like to hear it."

"Your mother probably had her own reasons for wanting Purdy to work with her horse. She chose to ignore the possibility of getting strangles, figuring the chances were small. Then, when the infection did show up, she was too embarrassed to own up to her mistake."

His scenario was more likely, Cassidy had to agree. But it still put the responsibility for the outbreak all on her mother. And it didn't change the fact that she had lied.

Chapter Fourteen

Farley left the café with Cassidy. Running into her this way had not been helpful to either the headache pounding behind his eyes or to his spirits, which felt as if they'd been dragged behind a herd of wild horses for a few days.

He'd been up early, wanting to arrange for Finnegan's burial as soon as possible. He'd also disinfected the barn so that Cassidy wouldn't have to face the heartbreak of doing it herself. It had seemed like the gentlemanly thing to do.

Out in the sunshine, standing beside the old truck that she was so ridiculously fond of, she thanked him.

"I slept in until noon. I can't remember the last time I did that. And when I finally made it down to the home barn, you'd taken care of everything. Thank you, Farley."

He had to look away, unable to bear how pretty she looked with the sunshine glinting like gold in her hair. She'd run out on him twice now. Only a fool would risk that kind of humiliation a third time.

"Don't worry about it. It's part of the job when you're a vet."

He saw that his comment wounded her, but hell, what did she expect from him?

"Look—I'm sorry about running out last night. You must have thought I was crazy."

"You'd had a rough night. And for the record—I wasn't trying to take advantage of that."

"Of course you weren't…"

"Good. I'm glad that's clear." His anger was coming through in his voice. He didn't intend it, but couldn't seem to stop it, either.

"It is," she said softly.

"Well, I'd better get going. I have a busy day."

She nodded.

He hesitated. "I hope you get that job, Cass. To hell with what your family thinks. You have to go after what you want in life."

Last night he'd been crazy enough to think that what he wanted was her.

But he needed a woman with a little more staying power.

ON THE DRIVE home from town Cassidy noticed something strange. The flowers on Brock's roadside marker were brown and neglected. This was the first time, in her knowledge, that they'd been left to molder. She parked on the side of the road and waded through the grass. When she arrived, she paused for a moment, with her head lowered and her heart aching.

Brock. We miss you.

Then she lifted the wreath off the marker. Immediately the dead blossoms began to disintegrate, scattering in the breeze, until Cassidy was left with only a few dried stems in her hand. She brushed them off into the grass, then went back to her truck.

Obviously Maddie had stopped tending her roadside tribute. But why?

HER FAMILY DIDN'T return from moving the cattle until it was almost dark that evening. Cassidy was waiting outside the barn. For some reason her mother had left Lucy behind and Cassidy had passed the time by setting up a barrel racing course and running Lucy through it.

No wonder the palomino had taken to the sport so quickly. Cassidy laughed at herself now, how she'd congratulated herself for being such a great teacher.

But she hadn't been the first to introduce Lucy to a barrel racing course. That would have been Joe Purdy.

Once the initial shock of discovering that her mother had purposefully exposed their horse to strangles had passed, Cassidy had started to wonder about why her mother would want Lucy trained in barrel racing in the first place.

Once again the puzzle pieces came together too easily.

Probably Olive hoped that barrel racing was another lure she could use to reel her daughter back in to Coffee Creek. A beautiful horse like Lucy—practically ideal for barrel racing? What horse-loving woman could resist?

Really, Olive had played all her cards, not leaving anything to chance. She wouldn't be pleased to find out that she had lost anyway.

Around five o'clock Cassidy groomed Lucy and let her out with the other horses, then she cleaned the arena, and finally she and Sky sat down to wait.

At quarter to six the posse of riders was visible coming down from the north. Cassidy watched until the moving blob turned into individual riders, then identifiable faces. When they finally came up to the barn, she could tell they were all exhausted.

Still, she showed no mercy.

"Finnegan died."

Everyone was silent for a moment, then Corb shook his head. "I'm sorry to hear that. When did it happen?"

"Last night. Farley's already had him buried. The barn's been disinfected and our quarantine is lifted."

"Finn was a good horse, but he was old," Olive said. "I know you did everything you could for him. At least this ordeal is behind us now."

"And who should we thank for that, Mother?"

Olive swung out of her saddle and handed the reins to Dave, who'd come out to help with the horses. Dave led the tired horse into the barn for grooming.

The other two wranglers, Eric and Jay, followed.

That left Corb, Jackson and Olive. Her brother and her mother were gaping at her with surprise. Jackson just looked as though he wanted to escape. When he tried to leave with the other cowboys, Cassidy stopped him by grabbing his arm.

"Please stay a minute. I'd like to get your input on something."

"Sure," he said cautiously. "I'm sorry about your horse. I know how much you loved Finnegan."

"Thanks, Jackson." She blinked away tears. This wasn't the time to be soft.

Speaking slowly and careful not to raise her voice, Cassidy recounted the information Straws had passed on to her at the Cinnamon Stick Café.

"Is it true, Mom? Did you know Joe Purdy had strangles on his ranch when you took Lucy to him for training?"

Olive's face had been growing progressively paler. Her eyes darted from her daughter's face, to her son's. Then finally to Jackson's.

Undoubtedly she was remembering his earlier assertion that he'd seen her loading Lucy into a trailer. She'd managed to discredit him the first time he'd said it. But this time it wouldn't be so easy.

After almost a minute of silence, she drew her breath.

"You're right. I took a risk that I shouldn't have. It was supposed to be a surprise for you, Cassidy. I originally bought Lucy to give to you as a graduation gift. Remembering how much you loved barrel racing I thought it would be fun to get her a little up-front training."

Despite her resolve to be firm and unyielding, Cassidy felt a little piece of her heart soften at this. Her mom had been right about one thing. She loved Lucy and couldn't have selected a more perfect horse for herself.

"But why risk her getting strangles? You could have taken her to Straws if getting her some training was so important to you."

"I wanted this to be a secret and I was worried someone at Monahan's would blab. You know how fast news travels in Coffee Creek."

The first part of her mother's explanation had tweaked her heart strings. But this—it just didn't make sense. Again, the risk, for a smart business person like her mother, just wouldn't have been worth it.

Unless it had been a calculated risk.

"You knew that a young, healthy horse like Lucy would almost certainly recover completely from a bout of strangles, didn't you?"

"Cassidy! Are you suggesting I *wanted* Lucy to get sick?"

Corb looked as shocked as Olive sounded. But Jackson, Cassidy noticed, didn't seem surprised at all by the suggestion.

She met her mother's gaze again, and in that instant, she knew that she had to stop here. Spelling out the reasons why her mother might have done such a thing would not give her any satisfaction, and would undoubtedly create wounds that would take a long time to heal.

"Only you know the answer to that question, Mom."

Then she asked Jackson if they could talk for a few minutes.

CASSIDY AND JACKSON headed to the office at the front of the barn. Cassidy sank into the upholstered chair, leaving the one behind the desk for her foster brother.

"I was wondering if you knew what was up with Maddie Turner? She's stopped tending the flowers on Brock's wreath. I'd assume she figured it was time to let it go, except she left the dead ones in place and that just doesn't seem like something she would do."

Jackson rubbed the back of his head. He had to be tired, hungry and longing for a good shower. She appreciated that he had taken a few minutes to talk to her about this.

"Well, you're right," he finally said. "It isn't something Maddie would do. Not if she had a choice. But she's in the hospital in Great Falls. I drove her there myself the day before we left on the cattle drive."

"Is she going to be okay?"

"Not likely. It's lung cancer and they didn't catch it early."

"Oh, dear. Does Mother know?"

"Do you think she would care?"

Cassidy couldn't answer that question. After today she could only conclude that she didn't know her mother nearly as well as she'd thought.

"Who's looking after her animals?"

He hesitated. "Vince Butterfield."

"The baker?" This just got stranger and stranger.

Jackson nodded again. "I don't know how he found out she was sick, but he's the one who asked me to drive her to the hospital. Apparently she wouldn't let him do it. But while she's gone, he plans to finish her roof and take care of the animals. She doesn't have a lot left. Mostly pets and about a dozen cattle."

Cassidy remembered how hard her mother had worked to convince Vince to come to their family dinner. He'd turned her down flat. And yet he'd rearranged his entire life in order to help Olive's sister.

"Thanks for telling me that, Jackson. Do you think they'd let me visit her in the hospital?"

He thought about it for a moment. "You're family. Why not?"

CASSIDY HEADED BACK to the house then and found her mother sitting on the open tailgate of Cassidy's old Ford.

"What's this?" Olive asked, waving at the boxes and suitcases in the back.

Earlier in the day Cassidy had packed her things, knowing that she couldn't wait until she'd heard about the job in Billings to start making changes in her life.

"I'm going to move, Mom. Into my own place. I know Brock's cabin is vacant. I'd like to stay there for Sky's sake. And I'll pay rent."

"Rent? Your brothers never paid rent, why should you? But moving into Brock's cabin is ridiculous. The house is plenty big enough for both of us. You don't really blame me for the strangles, do you?"

And truly, at that moment, Olive looked so small and vulnerable that it was almost impossible to believe.

"Besides," she added, her voice trembling a little, "we just redecorated your room."

Cassidy had expected her mother to take this tack. And while it was still effective, she'd prepared herself to handle it. "The room is beautiful, yes, but I warned you at the time I wouldn't be staying long."

Cassidy could tell her mother didn't know what to say. She'd done everything she could, played every card in her deck of tricks, but it wasn't working. She wanted Cassidy here, living with her. She wanted her working on the ranch and being the treasurer for the Heritage Committee. And, eventually, she wanted her to marry Dan Farley.

"This is crazy, honey." Olive raked a hand through her thick silver-blond hair. "I was planning to offer Brock's cottage to Winnie."

Cassidy didn't argue, even though she knew Corb had suggested this very thing, only to have Olive shoot down the suggestion. He'd also raised the idea of giving Winnie a cash settlement worth at least a portion of Brock's estate. After all, if Brock had died just two hours later, Winnie would have been his wife and entitled to everything.

But Olive was almost pathologically opposed to any part of the ranch going to someone who wasn't "family." Of course Winnie now had a son who was family. So maybe that was why she'd decided to make a gift of the cottage.

"I'm fine with that, Mom. Go ahead and give the cabin to Winnie and I'll ask her if I can rent the apartment over the Cinnamon Stick."

"Oh, for heaven's sake! Move into the cabin then. Who knows when Winnie Hayes will be back in town, anyway. Maybe never."

"Are you sure, Mom? 'Cause I don't mind—"

"I'm sure," she snapped. Then she shook her head. "What has gotten into you, daughter?"

There were lots of answers to that question. Some Olive would have found quite unkind. So Cassidy stuck with the obvious. "I've just grown up. That's all."

THAT SUNDAY CASSIDY drove into Great Falls to visit her aunt. When she gave her name and explained that she was a niece, she was allowed to visit her in the semi-private room.

She'd brought flowers. A vase of pretty tulips. It seemed the least she could do for a woman who had tended her brother's roadside memorial so faithfully, for so long.

"Cassidy. This is a surprise."

Maddie was sitting upright in her bed, connected to an intravenous line and dressed in a blue cotton gown. Her face looked gaunt and her hair grayer than ever, but her eyes were still that beautiful green.

"Jackson told me you were sick. I'm so sorry."

"Sit down. And thank you for the flowers. I've always loved tulips."

A curtain shielded the other patient from Cassidy's view, but she heard an older woman's husky voice say, "Me, too. Put them where we can both see them, love."

"Cassidy, meet June," Maddie said. "My partner in misery."

"Hey, June. Nice to meet you. How about I put the flowers here on the ledge at the back of the room. That way, when the curtain is pulled back, both of you can enjoy them."

"Nice to meet you, too, Cassidy. I've heard all about

you. But don't pull back the curtain now, love. I'm not decent back here."

June had heard all about her? Cassidy wasn't sure what to make of that. Had Maddie told her *everything* about their family?

"Seems you lucked out with your neighbor," she commented to her aunt and Maddie smiled.

"Indeed. It's wonderful to have someone to talk to."

"Maybe you'd like to talk to me, too, now that I'm here?"

"Why, of course. What would you like to talk about?"

"I'd like to know what the big family feud is about. What in the world happened, Aunt Maddie?"

It was the first time she'd ever linked those two words together. The effect was touching. Her aunt's eyes fluttered and tears blossomed like heavy dew drops.

"Oh, Cassidy. There aren't enough words… Have you tried talking to your mother?"

"I can't. But I've heard that she's angry because you wouldn't let her see her father before he died."

Maddie sighed and turned her head ever so slightly away. "Yes. I suppose that's the story."

"But you wouldn't do that, would you?" Even as she asked the question, Cassidy knew the answer was no. She could see the genuine pain in her aunt's eyes.

Her aunt was silent for at least a minute. And when she finally spoke again, her voice held a core of steel resolve. "I've been given six months, Cassidy. I don't want to end my days by spreading more discord among the family. It means a lot to me that you came to visit. Thank you."

"That's it? You're not going to tell me *anything?*"

"I can't, sweetheart. It really is better this way."

Chapter Fifteen

Farley was shoeing the first horse of the afternoon at the Monahans' place on Wednesday afternoon when he heard a familiar-sounding voice.

"Come this way, baby. That's a girl."

She sounded so much like Cassidy, he stepped out from the stalls with his alligator clinchers still in hand. There was a round arena right in front of the barn and sure enough, Cassidy was at the center of the pen working with a frisky bay mare.

With a wide-legged gait to accommodate the farrier chaps protecting his thighs, he started toward the fence. Cassidy had on her working boots and jeans, a pale pink tank top and her white hat. She must have stripped off her shirt earlier in the day. He could see it fluttering in the breeze from a fence post by the gate.

It was warm, that was for sure. There was a damp patch between her shoulder blades. And she paused to swipe the back of her arm over her forehead.

That was when she spotted him.

"Farley?" She let go of the lunge line. As she walked toward him, the gentled bay followed. As soon as she noticed, Cassidy smiled and paused. "Hey, girl, you're getting the idea now, aren't you? Here's your carrot. Hang on a minute now while I talk to my friend."

Disregarding the gate, she climbed over the fence, hopping down to the earth-packed ground right beside him.

"Hey, Farley." Her gaze swept over his chaps and the tool in his hand. "Shoeing some horses today?"

He nodded. "Les Felding and I just started the first one. How about you? What are you doing here?"

Whatever she was doing, she looked good. Like she belonged. An equine training center was the perfect place for someone like Cassidy and he wondered why he hadn't realized that before. A faint hope kindled in him as he waited for her answer.

"When I ran into Straws the other day at the café he said they'd just lost one of their instructors. I called him up later and told him I could help him out for a while. He has me working with some of their new young horses this week. Starting Monday he wants me to run a barrel racing camp for middle-grade girls. By the time that's over, hopefully I'll be starting my new job."

"In Billings?"

"Yeah. I haven't heard yet. But my fingers are crossed."

He should have known. When the hell was he going to stop being such a fool over this woman? The pretty receptionist at Monahan's front office had flirted daringly with him earlier. He should have asked her out.

Cassidy shuffled her boots in the dirt, then glanced up at him, almost shyly. "This is quite the operation, isn't it?"

"Straws runs a first-class outfit. Some of the top names in rodeo have been to his clinics. I'm going to the steer wrestling one next Sunday."

"Preparing for the Wild Rogue?"

"Yeah. B.J. called me on the weekend and confirmed

our plans. He's registering in the saddle bronc event and tie-down roping."

"He'll be after the big purse." Cassidy looked proud of her older brother.

Farley hesitated. He should leave it at that. But in the end, he couldn't stop himself from adding, "B.J. wants you to come, too."

He saw a wistful yearning cross her face, just seconds before she shook her head. "If I get the job I won't be able to take the time off. And I'd have no time or place to practice."

She was pretty quick with her excuses. Frankly, he was just as glad. "What does your mother think about you working here?"

"She isn't impressed. But her opinions don't sway me, anymore."

She said this definitively, and he realized that Olive had finally crossed a line that had changed everything between mother and daughter.

"You still living at the house?"

She shook her head. "In Brock's cabin. I was tempted to move into town, but that would have been tough on Sky. Coffee Creek Ranch is the only home she knows. I wish I could take her with me when I go to Billings. But I've thought about what you said and I realize that wouldn't be fair. She was happy with Corb and Laurel before. They'll give her a good home."

He fought back the urge to tell her that there was another solution here, staring her right in the face. She had to know how he felt about her. How he couldn't stop feeling about her. He knew he was being a fool, but there was just no choice. Not for him.

He loved her. He felt as if he always had.

But even if she wasn't leaving Coffee Creek, she

would never feel the same way about him. She'd proven that when she ran out on him the other night.

Cassidy had her plans, and she'd never wavered from them.

And maybe he should be grateful she was going to move to the city. If he couldn't have her, it would be easier this way. Perhaps one day he'd forget her enough to fall in love with someone else.

Then again, she'd been out of his life for four years and he'd come undone after just one look at her at the Cinnamon Stick Café.

"Farley, I want to apologize again for everything me and my family put you through."

"You don't need to apologize for your family. It was you who walked out the door after we made love. Not your mother or your brothers. You."

There. He'd put it to her plain.

She winced. "I was upset. I'd lost my horse, and—"

"Sure, you were upset. And for a while I worried that I may have taken advantage of that. But I don't think so anymore. I think *you* took advantage of *me*. Maybe you thought having sex would make the pain go away for a while. But it wasn't a diversion for me."

Her eyes were huge as she stared up at him. "Farley, I—"

"It's good that you're moving to Billings. I think a little distance from you is just what I need right now."

Tears started to build in her eyes, and his gut clenched at the sight. Damn her for knowing just how to get to him.

"I'm sorry if I hurt you. If you're trying to do the same to me, I have to tell you it's working."

He resisted the urge to wipe away the tears. To hold out his arms. "This isn't about hurting you. It's about me not being someone to help you pass the time until you hear from that damn accounting firm."

"No." She grabbed his arm and held on tight. "You were never that. You mean so much to me, Farley. Can't you see it in my eyes?"

For a second he almost believed her. But then the fates intervened and saved him from himself.

"Hey, Doc," an irritated voice called out from the stables. "You planning to shoe all four of this here horse's hoofs? Or just the one?"

"Be right there, Les." Farley pulled away, then angled his body back toward the stables, giving her one last look over his shoulder. She hadn't started back to the arena yet. She was still looking at him, her expression almost…wistful?

"See you around, Cass."

"Yes. See you around."

CASSIDY DIDN'T KNOW why she spent more time that afternoon reliving the encounter with Farley than she did checking her phone for messages from Cushman and Green. She felt as if there was something left unsaid between them and it worried her.

He'd done so much to help her since she'd come home. He'd fixed up Sky after the coyote attack, and he'd been there for her when Finnegan died, too.

He'd been the only one to offer the support she'd needed then. And what had happened after, well, it had been magical and she couldn't understand herself, why she had felt the urge to go home after.

He'd thought she was running from him.

But maybe she'd been running from herself and feelings that were just too big for her to contain.

The end result was that she had spoiled things between them again. And all she had to hold herself together was her work at Monahan's.

She really loved it. At the end of her second week, she was amazed by the progress her teenage girls had made with their horses. Their parents were pleased, too, and so was Straws.

"All of them would sign up on the spot for a second session if I could confirm that you would be the instructor," he told her on Thursday, as he passed over her check.

Cassidy folded the paper in half and tucked it into her back pocket. "It was so much fun. Some of those girls are really talented and there were a few great horses, too. But I can't promise anything beyond tomorrow, Mr. Monahan."

Back at home she ate her dinner outside, sitting in one of the wooden deck chairs looking at the lake, Sky at her feet, still damp from a quick swim.

In the distance, she heard Laurel call for Corb to come inside for dinner. She and Stephanie had returned yesterday from their visit to Winnie's family farm in Highwood. Apparently Winnie still wasn't ready to come back, though she would one day, since she'd invested all her money in the Cinnamon Stick Café and couldn't afford to sell.

Cassidy picked at the pizza she'd heated for her dinner. Despite the hard work she put in every day, she didn't have much appetite lately. She hadn't been sleeping well, either.

She supposed she was just nervous about the job. Twenty times a day she checked her phone for messages, and every night she logged on to Facebook to see if any of her classmates had been offered jobs. But all week there'd been no word. Everyone seemed to assume that she and Josh were shoo-ins, it was only the third person who was up for debate.

Cassidy wished she could feel as confident. She kept thinking over her interview and second-guessing things she'd said and done.

She laid the unfinished slice of pizza back on her plate and wondered what Farley was doing tonight. Maybe he'd gone back to dating Amber?

She should be glad for him if he had. After all, it was partly her fault that the relationship had broken apart when it did.

But the mental picture of him and Amber together didn't make her feel glad. She felt—*okay, face it*—jealous. She'd told herself that making love with him had been a terrible misstep.

The more she thought about it, though, the less like a mistake it seemed.

But that was a crazy way to think. Farley was part of the plan that her mother had made for her life. And she wasn't doing that anymore, letting Olive control her destiny.

Besides, Farley had made it pretty clear that he was done with her.

Cassidy started back for the cabin with Sky at her side. She'd feel better once she heard about the job. It was probably just the suspense of waiting that was making her so unsettled.

THE CALL CAME on Friday. As soon as she hung up, Cassidy paused to let it soak in. She'd been offered the job. Shouldn't she feel elated?

But she'd been through this before, when she'd applied for college and waited to see if she'd be accepted. She'd anticipated the acceptance letter would send her through the roof with excitement, but instead all she'd felt was satisfied and relieved.

Like she did right now.

Cassidy phoned her mom and her brothers to pass on the news. She had to leave messages for all of them; only Corb answered and professed that he was proud of her.

She doubted that she would have received such a civil comment from her mother.

When she'd finished the calls, she picked up the phone, hesitating over another number. She really wanted to tell Farley. But she was pretty sure he didn't want to hear from her.

So instead of phoning Farley she logged on to Facebook and checked her friends' status feeds. Within five minutes the news had been posted. Both Josh Brown and another one of their classmates, Adrienne Itani, had made the final cut. Cassidy confirmed her own good news, then sat back and thought about everything she had to do.

They'd been asked to start work the following Monday. Which meant she had the weekend to drive to Billings, find an apartment and buy some office-appropriate clothing, at least enough for a week.

She looked down at her hands, the calluses, the dirt beneath her nails that was always so hard to clean out. Maybe she should get those fancy gel nails, too.

It was hell leaving Sky. Corb and Laurel promised to take good care of her, though, and to give her lots of love. Leaving Lucy was almost as hard. Even though her mother's motives for buying the palomino were suspect, Cassidy and the horse had developed an amazing rapport.

Leaving her mother was not so hard. Cassidy had moved past her anger into a cooler place where she could still appreciate all that her mother had done for her, while, at the same time, freeing herself of the burden of trying to please Olive and make her proud.

So when her mother turned on the tears, Cassidy refused to be swayed into feeling guilty. She said her farewells, hugged and kissed her family, who had gathered at the porch to say goodbye, then headed for her truck.

A bark from Sky was the only thing that made her cry. She turned for a final look at her dog, then got behind the wheel and drove straight through to Billings without stopping.

She'd done some searching on the Net and had three appointments set up to look at apartments. She chose one on the ground floor of a lovely brick complex, only eight blocks from her office.

Next she went shopping and found a new suit, skirt and several blouses to mix and match.

And then it was her first day. She could hardly sleep the night before, and arrived at the office fifteen minutes early. Josh arrived next, and she was shocked at how little she felt when she saw him.

He gave her a hug and told her he'd missed her.

But inside all she had was a big void.

Adrienne came next, one minute before nine and Cassidy was awed by how professional and elegant she looked. She was wearing a similar outfit to Cassidy— skirt, jacket and blouse. Yet Adrienne wore them with a natural grace that Cassidy just didn't feel.

They were given an orientation by Pamela. Then introduced to the managers under whom they'd be working. The first day involved reviewing manuals and signing lots of paperwork. On Tuesday they were assigned clients and reviewed files and given jobs of photocopying papers and making up schedules. Wednesday Cassidy accompanied her manager to her first client meeting. Thursday she was put to work finding documentation for certain expense transactions, a job that continued to Friday and, she was told, would probably take her the rest of the next week to complete.

Cassidy felt her spirits drop. The job was turning out so different from what she'd expected. She glanced out the window. The blue sky teased her. She wondered about her family, her dog and her horse. Mostly, she wondered about Farley. Was he missing her at all?

ANGER DROVE FARLEY for several days after Cassidy left Coffee Creek. The damned woman had toyed with him like he was a mouse.

Again.

And he'd let her.

What the hell was wrong with him?

By Thursday, that story wasn't washing anymore. After dinner, when he was out walking with his dogs, he finally admitted the truth. Cassidy wasn't into manipulating or playing games. If she'd slept with him, it had to have meant something to her.

Trouble was, the meaning had been inconvenient. It hadn't fit into her plan.

And so she'd run.

And what had he done? Taken offense and pulled back.

Never once had he told her how he really felt about her. Never once had he put his heart—and his pride—on the line and said the words.

Once, he'd told her that if she wanted something, she should go after it.

Didn't the same advice apply to him?

Farley went into the office to check his appointments for the next day. As usual his schedule was booked solid.

He could always wait for Saturday. But his gut told him no. It had to be tomorrow.

He slashed a black line through his afternoon appointments. Liz would make the phone calls for him.

After lunch, he'd be on the road.

FRIDAY AT FIVE, they were all back at the office. Cassidy had never been so happy to see the end of a work week.

"We have to hit the bar," Josh said, clearing off his workstation.

"Absolutely," Adrienne agreed. "My manager tells me a lot of the first and second years go to the Irish pub on the corner. How does that sound?"

"Good with me," Josh said. "Cass, you coming?"

She walked by the Silver Unicorn every day to and from work. It was a dark, low-ceilinged place. No outside patio. She was longing for sunshine and clean air, but she said yes anyway, just to be sociable.

Her stomach was churning as they rode the elevator down to the lobby level. She'd been on edge all week, anxious to do a good job and, more important, not screw up.

But that desire to perform well had hidden other feelings. Something awful was swelling and intensifying inside of her. She didn't know what it was. But even breathing seemed to be harder with each passing second.

As soon as she stepped out of the revolving door to the street, Cassidy realized that the feeling she'd been unable to name was suffocation.

She hated the new job. Just hated it.

She didn't like the city, the sidewalks, the pollution or the noise.

How could she have done this? She'd studied so hard for her degree. She'd dedicated the past five years to it.

And yet, now that her goal was in hand, she'd never been so unhappy.

She took a deep breath and knew that she couldn't go to the pub tonight.

She couldn't go back to the office on Monday, either. She was no quitter, but there was no sense in spending her life in a place where she didn't belong. It was really as simple as that.

Josh and Adrienne were still by her side. She didn't know what to tell them. But suddenly Adrienne stopped. "Wow. Check out that cowboy at eleven o'clock. Is he hot, or what?"

Cassidy looked.

Adrienne had spotted one hot cowboy all right. He was tall and broad-shouldered, dressed entirely in black, leaning against a concrete pillar, one cowboy boot crossed casually over the other.

As soon as her gaze landed on him, he touched the brim of his hat in acknowledgment.

"My, oh, my." Adrienne patted a hand over her sleek brown hair. "He's looking right at me as if he knows me or something."

"He's hot all right," Cassidy agreed. "But he's mine."

She reached down and took off the high-heeled shoes that had started blisters on the back of her heels. In bare feet she walked over the hot concrete path and dropped the shoes into a handy trash can. *Good riddance to you.*

"Way to go, sister," cheered a woman wearing white running shoes with her suit.

Cassidy smiled, but kept walking in a line that would take her straight to Farley. He was the last person she'd ever expected to see here.

But, she now realized, he was also the only one she really wanted.

With every step she drew closer to him. And he was smiling. Momentarily she felt a pang of sorrow for all she was leaving behind. She'd had so many hopes and aspirations.

But she saw now that it had never been something she wanted. Only something her mother didn't want her to want.

She'd spent the past five years in a pretty confused state. Between trying to think for herself and avoid her mother's attempts at manipulation, she'd forgotten to do the most important thing.

Follow her heart.

When she reached him, Farley held out his arms and swept her feet right off the ground.

"I missed you," he said. "And I've come to get you. But only if you're ready to be mine. No more running."

She looked into his eyes, so steadfast, so true. There was something powerful between them, and it had been there from the start. At twenty-one it had scared her. But now she understood that far from being subsumed by it, she would be made stronger by it and more fulfilled.

"I love you, Farley."

And then he kissed her.

Epilogue

It was Saturday night at the Wild Rogue Rodeo in Central Point, Oregon. Steer wrestling was just a hobby for Farley, something he did for a change of pace from the relentless hard work of his veterinary practice.

Although he'd brushed up on his skills at the steer wrestling clinic at Monahan's, he hadn't really expected to place at the rodeo. He was just here for fun and the companionship of some people who meant a lot to him.

But he'd done unexpectedly well on Thursday and Friday. And if he did as well tonight, he'd go home with some money. And maybe even a trophy.

But all of that was just gravy to him now.

The announcer was calling his name. "Next up we have Dan Farley, a vet from Coffee Creek, Montana, here to show us that he has a few bulldogging skills, as well…"

The voice faded as Farley concentrated on what he was doing. B.J. Lambert had agreed to be his hazer and he was on the other side of the chute where the steer would momentarily be running from. B.J. would keep that steer moving in a straight line. The rest was up to him.

He urged his mount into position. At the same time

he heard a sweet voice holler from the crowd. "You can do it, Farley!"

Cassidy. She was waving her hat, her blond hair blowing crazily in the breeze.

His back went straighter, his head prouder. With a girl like Cassidy Lambert cheering for him, how could he ever fail?

He gave a nod and the chute man tripped the lever. Out raced the revved-up longhorn—six hundred pounds of him, in Farley's estimation.

The second the barrier released, Farley was off, too. His horse was a dream, bringing him right up to the sweet zone. With a leap of faith he leaned over his horse and grabbed for the steer's horns. For a second he was out there—hanging in the air while his horse ran flat-out.

The next, he had an elbow crooked around one horn, a fist over the other.

He wasn't thinking or planning now, just moving on instinct. He felt his boots slip out of the stirrups and he slid to the left, pulling the steer's head until he had the nose nestled up in the crook of his arm.

The legs were up. The horn sounded.

"5.6 seconds!"

Farley released the steer, then found his footing. He was sure he could hear Cassidy cheering above the roar of the crowd. His time wouldn't win him any records. But it might just get him the top ranking for the night.

He brushed the dust from his legs, waved his hat at the crowd, then hurried out of the arena. His shoulders ached a lot. He was getting old for this sport. But what a rush.

CASSIDY WANTED TO find Farley and congratulate him on his performance. She was so proud of him. He'd been competing against some pretty serious cowboys tonight and he'd beat them all!

She hoped to do him proud, too, in the barrel racing event. But she also knew it wouldn't pay to set her expectations too high. She'd been doing a lot of training this past month at Monahan's—Straws had offered her a full-time position when he heard she'd quit the job in Billings—but she'd also been away from the sport for a long time.

And she'd never before competed in a bona fide PRCA sanctioned rodeo.

She wiped her hands nervously on her cream-colored jeans. She'd chosen a golden Western-styled shirt for her top, and her hat had a matching gold band. The colors worked perfectly with both her coloring and Lucy's.

Her mother had made her a gift of the horse when she came back from Billings. She'd been gracious about it, too, but then she'd been proven right, hadn't she?

It still galled Cassidy to admit it.

Her mother had known she belonged in the country. And she'd known Farley was the right man for her, as well. If she had only stepped back and let nature take its course, Cassidy figured she could have saved herself— and those she loved—from a lot of heartache and grief.

But stepping back was never going to be Olive's way.

And for good, and bad, her mother was a force in her life that she was always going to have to deal with.

Before Cassidy knew it, the barrel racing had started. She was the sixth and final contestant. She heard the excitement of the crowd as she and Lucy lined up at the gate.

"And here she is, the golden girl and her golden horse from Coffee Creek, Montana. Don't they make a pretty picture? This is Cassidy Lambert and her palomino Lucky Lucy. I'm betting Cassidy won't be needing any luck tonight. Not based on what we saw from her last night."

Cassidy was so nervous she thought she was going to be sick. And then she caught Farley's eyes, standing off to the side near the chutes for the bucking horses. He nodded at her, and she could almost hear his calm, strong voice inside her head.

"You're my girl, Cassidy. You can do anything."

And she felt that she could. His love took all the best things about her and made them better. She ran a hand down Lucy's neck, then leaned over to whisper in her ear. "Be my lucky girl. Let's go!"

Though it was well-known that Olive did not care for the rodeo, she went to Central Point, Oregon, that weekend to see her eldest son, daughter and soon-to-be son-in-law compete. That was one thing about her mom, Cassidy thought. She always put her kids first. And it did seem Olive was proud when Cassidy came in third for barrel racing. Farley placed first for steer wrestling and B.J. won both the saddle bronc and tie-down roping events, ending up the big winner of a thirty-five-thousand-dollar prize.

Olive congratulated them at the end of the ceremony, then excused herself. Much as she didn't like the rodeo, she especially hated the partying that went on afterward.

Cassidy and Farley, however, were happy to go to the Rogue Saloon and socialize with all the other competitors, with B.J. promising to follow once he'd given an interview to some local journalists.

At the saloon Cassidy and Farley did *some* socializing.

And then all Cassidy wanted was to dance with Farley.

He was holding her in his arms when a song came on that they both instantly recognized. For the first time that night she tripped. And Farley steadied her.

"You aren't going to run away this time, I hope?" he whispered in her ear.

It was the last song they'd danced to four years ago, before she'd panicked and sabotaged their date.

"I'm never running again," she promised him.

"I'll hold you to that." He brushed a thumb over the diamond ring he'd given her two weeks ago. "So—had any thoughts about when we should have the wedding?"

"Soon." She was anxious to move in with him, and figured Sky would adjust okay—she'd already been accepted as a pal by Tom and Dick.

"I'm good with that. Just give me a date so I can tell my folks. They'll want to book a flight."

"Are you okay with something small?"

"Whatever you want."

"Just close family and friends. I'd like it to be at the Coffee Creek Church."

"Are you sure?"

She nodded. Their family needed to purge the painful memories of Brock's wedding-that-never-happened. "And Straws told me we could have the reception in his dining room. It's beautiful and has such amazing views of the mountains."

"Have you talked to your mother about any of this?"

"Not yet. I want you with me when I do. She'll have a place of honor at the wedding as my mother, but I don't want her commandeering the plans, the way she tried to do with Laurel and Corb."

Farley remembered. Olive had organized every detail of that event, only to have the young couple elope in New York.

"I can handle Olive," he assured her. "You, now, that's a different story. You have me wrapped around your little finger. You know that, right?"

She laughed. She'd never been so happy. "I plan to keep you there, too, cowboy. And don't forget it."

* * * * *

Be sure to come back to Coffee Creek, Montana, in July 2013 when B.J. Lambert returns to the family ranch in C.J. Carmichael's next American Romance novel, PROMISE FROM A COWBOY!

REQUEST YOUR FREE BOOKS!
2 FREE NOVELS PLUS 2 FREE GIFTS!

HARLEQUIN

American ★ *Romance*®

LOVE, HOME & HAPPINESS

YES! Please send me 2 FREE Harlequin® American Romance® novels and my 2 FREE gifts (gifts are worth about $10). After receiving them, if I don't wish to receive any more books, I can return the shipping statement marked "cancel." If I don't cancel, I will receive 4 brand-new novels every month and be billed just $4.49 per book in the U.S. or $5.24 per book in Canada. That's a savings of at least 14% off the cover price! It's quite a bargain! Shipping and handling is just 50¢ per book in the U.S. and 75¢ per book in Canada.* I understand that accepting the 2 free books and gifts places me under no obligation to buy anything. I can always return a shipment and cancel at any time. Even if I never buy another book, the two free books and gifts are mine to keep forever.

154/354 HDN FVPK

Name _____ (PLEASE PRINT) _____

Address _____ Apt. # _____

City _____ State/Prov. _____ Zip/Postal Code _____

Signature (if under 18, a parent or guardian must sign) _____

Mail to the **Harlequin® Reader Service:**
IN U.S.A.: P.O. Box 1867, Buffalo, NY 14240-1867
IN CANADA: P.O. Box 609, Fort Erie, Ontario L2A 5X3

Want to try two free books from another line?
Call 1-800-873-8635 or visit www.ReaderService.com.

* Terms and prices subject to change without notice. Prices do not include applicable taxes. Sales tax applicable in N.Y. Canadian residents will be charged applicable taxes. Offer not valid in Quebec. This offer is limited to one order per household. Not valid for current subscribers to Harlequin American Romance books. All orders subject to credit approval. Credit or debit balances in a customer's account(s) may be offset by any other outstanding balance owed by or to the customer. Please allow 4 to 6 weeks for delivery. Offer available while quantities last.

Your Privacy—The Harlequin® Reader Service is committed to protecting your privacy. Our Privacy Policy is available online at www.ReaderService.com or upon request from the Harlequin Reader Service.

We make a portion of our mailing list available to reputable third parties that offer products we believe may interest you. If you prefer that we not exchange your name with third parties, or if you wish to clarify or modify your communication preferences, please visit us at www.ReaderService.com/consumerschoice or write to us at Harlequin Reader Service Preference Service, P.O. Box 9062, Buffalo, NY 14269. Include your complete name and address.

HARI3

SPECIAL EXCERPT FROM

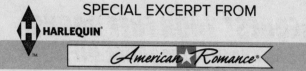

HARLEQUIN®

American ★ Romance®

The Texas Lawman's Woman

by Cathy Gillen Thacker

Welcome to Laramie County, Texas,
where you're bound to run into the first
man you ever loved....

Shelley Meyerson's heart leaped as she caught sight of the broad-shouldered lawman walking out of the dressing room. She blinked, so shocked she nearly fell off the pedestal. "*He's* the best man?"

Colt McCabe locked eyes with Shelley, looking about as pleased as Shelley felt. His chiseled jaw clenched. "Don't tell me *she's* the maid of honor!"

"Now, now, you two," their mutual friend, wedding planner Patricia Wilson, scolded, checking out the fit of Shelley's yellow silk bridesmaid dress. "Surely you can get along for a few days. After all, you're going to have to...since you're both living in Laramie County again."

Don't remind me, Shelley thought with a dramatic sigh.

Looking as handsome as ever in a black tuxedo and pleated white shirt, Colt sized Shelley up. "She's never going to forgive me."

For good reason, Shelley mused, remembering the hurt and humiliation she had suffered as if it were yesterday. She whirled toward Colt so quickly the seamstress stabbed her with a pin. But the pain in her ribs was nothing compared to the pain in her heart. She lifted up her skirt, revealing her favorite pair of cranberry-red cowgirl boots, and stomped off the pedestal, not stopping until they were toe to toe. "You stood me up on prom night, you big galoot!"

Lips thinning, the big, strapping lawman rocked forward on the toes of his boots. "I got there."

Yes, he certainly had, Shelley thought. And even that had been the stuff of Laramie, Texas, legend. The town had talked about it for weeks and weeks. "Two hours late. Unshowered. Unshaven." Shelley threw up her hands in exasperation. "No flowers. No tuxedo…."

Because if he had looked then the way he looked now… Well, who knew what would have happened?

Read more of *THE TEXAS LAWMAN'S WOMAN* this May 2013, and watch for the rest of this new miniseries McCABE HOMECOMING by Cathy Gillen Thacker. Only from Harlequin® American Romance®!

HAREXPO513